Melissa —

When You Truly
After It Without Limiting Yourself With
Disbelief The Universe Will Make It
Happen.

The Emerald Chant

By Will

By

Bryston Williams

Copyrights

All trademarks are of their respective owners. Rather than put a trademark symbol after every occurrence of a trademarked name, we use names in an editorial fashion only, and to the benefit of the trademark owner, with no intention of infringement of the trademark. Where such designations appear in this book, they have been printed with initial caps.

The purpose of this report is to educate. The author and publisher do not warrant that the information contained in this book is fully complete and shall not be responsible for any errors or omissions. The author and publisher shall have neither liability nor responsibility to any person or entity with respect to any loss or damage caused or alleged to be caused directly or indirectly by this book, nor do we make any claims or promises of your ability to generate income by using any of this information.

Part 1

There was a boy named Itabi who wished he had a different name. The other children in his clan all had names that fit. They did not get laughed at and nobody gave them funny looks. But Itabi was different. He knew his mother had named him after the howling of the wolves but he still wondered why she did it. He knew because his grandmother had told him the story a thousand times. His mother, Opa, had left Chucalissa to give birth next to the peacefulness of a running creek, as per the custom of their people. Opa hadn't slept the night before—a pack of wolves nearby had kept her awake. No one heard them but her.

The meadow became a blur as he squinted at the dragonflies dancing over patches of strawberries.

As Opa laid there in the shade of a sycamore tree, she noticed footprints in the sand. They were in the shape of wolf paws and surrounded her. The name of her newborn became obvious, as all true things do, and so it was that the boy's story began.

The wings of the dragonflies now reflected the brilliance of the setting sun.

The boy longed for their freedom. He felt the same longing when he watched the smoke rise from the fires in front of the elders' huts.

Itabi. Ih-ta-bee.

It was a beautiful name, but there was a problem: the boy couldn't say it. He stumbled over the sounds, or repeated them many times before they came together. Ih-Ih-Ih. *Itabi.*

Words were his enemy. Whenever the boy wanted to summon them, his tongue rebelled. He listened to the chief of his clan, the Miko Colesqua, give speeches in the town square. The sound of his voice flowed like honey from tree-bark.

Words are the Miko's friend, the boy thought to himself. Why can't I make peace with them too?

Dusk spread its shawl across the woodlands and Itabi listened to the chorus of cicadas. All things in the world appeared beautiful when they understood their purpose.

The boy's grandfather had been the last medicine man of the Owl Clan. For as long as they could remember, even before their people had first arrived at the shores of the great river, the medicine man had passed down the secrets of healing to a chosen few.

Itabi's grandfather couldn't do that. One night during a howling thunderstorm, he lost his power of speech. His voice was never to appear again; in a flash of lightning, the wisdom of a thousand years was lost. The fortunes of Chucalissa had been in decline ever since. No one seemed to remember the old way of life.

Itabi had felt the weight of the clan's hopes on his shoulders since he was a boy. Maybe the rays of the sun would grant him the memories of his grandfather, the people speculated and hoped. They saw, however, that the boy's words faltered on his lips and he lagged behind other boys in the skill of hunting. It had to be a curse, they reasoned.

The boy still remembered how his grandfather dressed for ceremonies. He wore moccasins made of white deerskin tipped with eagle claws and a tuft of owl feathers fanned from his crown. He blessed seven kernels of corn for the harvest and then raised his arms in reverence over the sacred fire. His wisdom, for a time, hadn't needed words to speak to the people's hearts.

Itabi wondered ruefully if he could ever achieve something like that. He had many thoughts and ideas, but they were like creatures without wings that could never take flight. He spoke very little around the people of his clan. He hated to see how their eyes fell in embarrassment as his tongue tripped over unfriendly syllables. They called him *hatak ikanumpolo* — a mute.

The boy remembered his recent interaction with the canoe-maker's daughter. His mother had instructed him to take some fresh logs of cypress to the canoe-maker as a favor. He did as instructed and as he bent down to unload the heavy wood from his cart, beautiful Talulah stepped through the doorway and stopped to watch him. Her hair streamed in torrents down her back and her eyes captured the glow of the Sun.

"Your m-moccasins, um–"

Itabi wanted her to notice that they were wearing the same tawny owl feathers on their leather moccasins. Talulah looked down in sudden concern, her hair falling into her face.

"What about them? Are you saying they're dirty?"

"N-no, I just mean…" Itabi desperately pointed at her moccasins and then at his own to indicate his meaning.

"…the same."

Talulah looked at him for a moment and then broke into laughter. "Yes brother, I'm sure that's what you meant!"

She ran off without giving Itabi another chance to respond. People never had the patience to listen to him. It took him longer to say what he wanted, but shouldn't that only make what he had to say more interesting? There were so many things he wanted to tell Talulah—none of them had anything to do with moccasins and owl feathers.

The sun had taken the dragonflies with it.

Itabi always wondered where they went after sundown. The boy liked to get away from the activity of Chucalissa and come to this meadow for solitude. He spent hours watching the breeze ripple through the wild grasses.

Was it destiny that had led his mother to hear those wolves? Could destiny be wrong? Itabi sighed. He wished he could speak to Talulah in the same way the breezes spoke to the meadow. Propping his head against an old sycamore and closing his eyes, Itabi resolved that one day he would do exactly that.

•

"The boy has no voice," Colesqua the Miko cried. *"What good is he to Fala?"*

The gathering of men seated in the chief's chamber was quiet for a moment. All eyes were trained on the motionless figure stretched out in the middle of the clay floor.

"We have no other choice, Miko," a younger man said gravely. *"He is Shikoba's grandson and the only one with a chance of remembering the old formulas."*

The chief of the Owl Clan gazed down at his daughter's supine body with ill-concealed emotion. Her fever had been raging for three days and her consciousness rarely surfaced. The people's memory of medicine had become entirely blank; even the elders were helpless to recall the old preparations.

"Have our ancestors not completely abandoned us? We are the People of One Fire, but our fires are now little more than embers in the ground! The life of our people is a flame too weak to be rekindled..." said Colesqua as he sat down next to his daughter's body.

Two of the men exchanged a look and a nod, and the second one swiftly withdrew from the chamber. Each person felt their grief for young Fala as a physical force that dragged their spirits downward. The force grew stronger in the silence.

"Someone must have the courage to say it, Great Miko," one of the warriors finally said. *"Our people have been struck by a curse. The magic of the Bear Clan's high priests is diabolical. Is there any doubt they are responsible for this...this plague?"*

"His words are true," said another. *"We know they have harbored resentment against us. Now we dip our*

feathers in red paint and proceed to battle, as in the days of legend."

Two figures entered the Miko's chamber, wordlessly interrupting the warriors. One of them was Itabi. All attention turned to the boy. He attempted to break away, but someone placed a heavy hand on his shoulder. Itabi's eyes widened when he caught sight of Colesqua's daughter.

"Itabi, grandson of Shikoba!" The Miko stood up and addressed the boy with a thundering sincerity. *"Your tribe needs you more than it ever has. My daughter lies on the edge of death. In her fate lies the fate of our people. Restore life to my Fala, in the name of our ancestors!"*

The boy did not understand why they had called him to the chief's lodge. Everybody knew Itabi had no gift to give to his people; there were no eagle talons at the tip of his moccasins. But that couldn't be true, Itabi told himself, it just *couldn't*. He stepped towards Fala. Everyone's eyes felt like arrows piercing his back.

Itabi remembered how his grandfather prayed to each of the four directions before working with the sick. He did this inaudibly, then knelt down next to the girl. She was wrapped in deerskin on a woven mat striped with the colors of the sunset. In his mind's eye, the boy could still see Fala bounding over the creek where the giant sycamore grew.

There was something that awoke within him like distant thunder, or like when a baby bird remembers it has wings. Something the boy's grandfather had said in his old incantations was coming through: *crown of the sky, father of waters, dancing daughter of four winds who brought the song of fire...*

"*Crown of–cr–crown of s-s–*"

Almost as soon as Itabi began his recitation, Fala's breaths began to come more sharply. A wave of consternation passed around the lodge. "*Faster!*" the Miko cried. "*You must speak faster, Itabi!*"

"*Father of w-waters–*"

A final current of breath went through the girl's body and her head slumped to the side in eternal rest. Everyone was too stunned to move for a moment. Itabi lived an entire lifetime in that brief interval, crouching there with Shikoba's words still half-formed on his lips.

Everything became a blur. Fala's mother fell upon her daughter's body with piercing wails. Someone lifted Itabi by the armpits and carried him from the Miko's lodge. Tears of fury raining down his cheeks, the boy began to yell at the top of his lungs.

"Dancing d-daughter who brought the song of fire! Dancing d-daughter..."

He blacked out before he could finish.

•

Tak-tak-tak!

Opa's forearms glistened with sweat as she pounded roots in a wooden mortar. Her efforts yielded a growing mountain of red powder at the bottom of the bowl. The roots had been hard to find that morning — harder than usual.

"Soon we shall forget how to prepare our meals too," Opa, a widow, muttered to herself.

Tak-tak-tak! Tak-tak-tak!

A head poked out of the lodge, took in the scene and withdrew again like a turtle disappearing into its shell. Opa shook her head and grimaced at her mortar.

"*Itabi! Are you too lazy to help your mother?*"

The boy came outside and sat next to her on the ground. He watched his mother pound the roots into powder and let the sound fill his ears. *Tak-tak-tak!* Neither spoke for several minutes.

"*The council of elders will see you today,*" Opa finally said.

"*Yes,*" Itabi flatly replied.

"*Will you be ready?*"

"*Hoke.*"

She looked at him for a moment. Then handed him a basket to hold out. Itabi watched vacantly as his mother emptied the powder into the basket and began pouring water over it to moisten it. He'd done his best to avoid conversation for several days, finding refuge in wordlessness.

"*Soon,*" Opa said, "*we'll have more jelly to go with those hot corn cakes you like so much.*"

"*We don't have any fire to make c...c...nobody does!*"

"*Hush, Itabi! There is still enough to fire the kettle —*"

The boy dropped the basket to the ground and stood up. *"I can't help that I'm s-so different. It's not my fault I'm ikanumpolo..."*

Opa put the mortar down and motioned him to come inside with her. The clay walls of their home soothed the heat of the morning sun. Opa studied her son's face and admired its blooming maturity. She understood things about Itabi that he didn't yet understand about himself.

"Let me tell you about how our people came to live here at Chucalissa," Opa started.

"But-"

The boy's mother put a silencing hand in the air.

"In the past, we were a people without a home. We wandered the mountains, forests and plains in search of a place we could call our own — but it was hard, Itabi. Not everyone made it. There are burial grounds we still don't know about, you see?

Finally, the medicine man took a long branch of oak and cut it into a single thin strip. He painted and then planted it as a pole in the ground. This is what he said to us: 'Every morning, check the pole to see in which direction it leans. If it leans strongly in one direction, that is the direction you travel. When it stands straight up, then you will know you have found your home.'

Our people traveled and traveled, and yet each morning the medicine man's pole leaned crooked. One morning they woke up and saw that it stood straight. Thus, we became hatcha hatak, the river people. We have lived here ever since."

The boy had heard the story many times. He struggled to see why his mother was telling it to him in this moment. Itabi looked at her quizzically.

"I don't know what decision the council will come to tonight, son. As your mother I must prepare myself for anything – that is my personal burden. Our people had to go on a journey to discover who they were, where they belonged in the world. You're a young man now. You must be prepared to do the same."

Itabi felt at once frightened and excited by his mother's unexpected words. He knew that a part of her yearned to roam the lands of their ancestors freely and that she had chosen to stay in Chucalissa as a woman of her tribe. But Itabi knew nothing of what existed beyond his clan and its territories and for the first time, he understood that such knowledge could change who he was.

As she sat there trying to read his thoughts, Opa remembered a complaint the boy had recently made to her. He was upset that people wouldn't let him finish his sentences. She reached over and cradled the boy's chin in the palm of her hand.

"They will listen to you, Itabi. Trust me, they will listen!"

•

Twilight fell on the *talwa* of Chucalissa and her town-square buzzed with activity. Everyone was moving towards the council house to hear what was to come of Shikoba's grandson. There were corn-harvesters, basket-weavers, ballplayers, sculptors and hunters. Their occupations were secondary to the responsibility they owed their clan.

Several hundred people were already inside. The Miko was seated at the center of the chamber, flanked by two of his advisors. A great pillar anchoring the roof stood behind the altar containing the sacred fire. Itabi, shifting in his seat, never took his eyes off the withering flame. No matter what it was fed, the fire remained frail and unimpressive.

As the last people filed in, the Miko of the Owl Clan motioned for silence. He wore a headdress of feathers with a pure white mantle and the sculpted face of an owl dangling from his neck. Colesqua began the meeting with disputes between wedded couples; Itabi expelled a sigh of relief. People lose a lot of time getting upset at small things, the boy thought to himself.

Fala's death had left the people distraught. She was thought of very highly throughout the clan as she had shown wisdom from a very young age. Days earlier she was buried with her emerald necklace around her neck under a summer day's blue skies. The Miko and his wife were in deep mourning but could not permit themselves to be lost in grief — the crisis of their people begged for their leadership.

"It is time..." the Miko announced. "...that we address a matter of grave importance."

Itabi felt the energy of the entire clan's attention shift toward him like a wave. He became conscious of his facial expression and the way he was sitting. His mother was seated at some distance from him and the boy felt an urge to run to her. His feet, however, were rooted to the spot.

"There was a time when the sacred fire was not like this. It was a proud, roaring flame. There was a time when we performed our ceremonies and healed our sick with no disturbance. Times are different now, and it is hard to understand why this has befallen our people.

Tonight, my daughter is with the elders in the sky. It would be unfair of me to blame anyone for not saving her. We all have done our best. It is in looking to our future, however, that we are confronted with losing more. Young Itabi, what have you to say?"

The boy described his experience that day the best he could. There was a flash, an inkling of the old way of healing; but his defect in speech prevented him from reciting the mantra. Tears came to his eyes; he was not sure if that was why they had lost her. Everyone felt pity for him.

"It is clear," the Miko said, *"that you have a good heart. You wish to follow the right way, but don't know how. I have spoken with the elders about this. Itabi, your place is not with us in Chucalissa. If you are to gain the power to heal our people, you must leave us to seek that power. The*

*council has spoken; anyone who would like to speak on this
matter can now do so."*

The boy watched the fragile ribbon of smoke as
it rose through the grass roof to meet the night sky.
The council has spoken. He felt a mixture of things in his
heart that confused him.

Chucalissa was the only place he'd ever known.
Even though they communicated exile, there was love
in Colesqua's words, too. The pride of being asked to
heal his clan, for a moment, overcame the feelings of
dejection from being sent away.

"I am compelled to be heard by the council," said a
warrior. *"Soon, war cries will fill the air and men will draw
their arrows in contempt. This council will dress in red, not
white. Is there any question as to why our oracles have gone
quiet, our medicine men useless? There is no use in sending
this troubled boy into the wilderness."*

"Yes," another said, *"if we are under attack, it is
better to keep the boy with us, Miko. It could be dangerous
to let him wander alone. It is not wise to risk such a thing."*

Itabi could feel how the warriors' warnings
reshaped the people's thoughts. The fear in their

words had spread to every person in the room. He saw how fear had the power to change the decisions people made. Peace was threatened by fear. To his surprise, the boy heard his mother's voice interject.

"My brothers, it is not a war we need, but a vision quest. The sacred fire is low because we are forgetting ourselves. War rarely gives an answer...only more questions! We will find our voice as a people when my son finds his. That is his path, I've seen it."

The Miko nodded and surveyed the room. Some of the warriors shook their heads but said nothing. The majority were in favor of Itabi leaving Chucalissa. Perhaps Fala was in favor too, the boy thought. His mother had spoken so strongly that he didn't doubt it. *A vision quest.* They exchanged a glance and Opa gave him a nod of encouragement.

"It is decided then," proclaimed Colesqua. *"The time has come for you to fulfill your name, Itabi."* The council-members nodded in agreement and soon the meeting was adjourned.

•

The person who starts on the path of dreams is not the same one who finishes it.

The boy had seen a green snake shimmer between the tall stalks of corn outside his home, and these were the strange words that first came to his mind. They had been whispered in his ear by someone as he left the council house that night—the boy hadn't seen who said it. He was walking with Opa in a small group; when he turned around, Itabi only saw the young son of his mother's friend.

Who could've said that?

The green snake moved like a ripple of water, disappearing into the cornfield.

The people of the Owl Clan saw the snake as a magical creature for the simple fact that it was never afraid to change into something new. His grandfather, Opa had told Itabi, had been able to speak with snakes. At least, they had stopped shedding their skins around the hut when he asked them to! His mother always giggled when she told the story.

Who would he be by the harvest moon? Would he become something he could be proud of? Would he, in the Miko's words, gain the power to heal the people of Chucalissa? Whatever happens on this journey, Itabi thought, it will certainly make me a different person from who I am now.

He suddenly felt a powerful wave of sadness overtake his entire being. I'm already becoming a stranger to who I am, the boy thought to himself. It struck him that everything he'd ever known was ready to slip into the past forever. His life as a boy in Chucalissa, his loving mother and her hot cakes, the strawberry meadow, all of the children he'd grown up with who even though they had never accepted him, were still a part of his life.

The fields of beans, corn and yams would go on existing, but they would only be a memory, just like everything else. The boy felt the desire to hang on to everything he knew, to stay just as he was. Itabi shook his head. He could feel some kind of force pulling him outward into the unknown. That was where he would meet a new Itabi, somewhere on the path of dreams.

Ever since that night of the council meeting, the boy kept having the same dream. In the dream, he walked on a path that went into the sky. He wanted to stop and turn around, but every time he thought about it, he saw Fala up ahead of him on the path. She would turn around and look at him, then run around the next bend. Itabi felt dizzy; lost in the stars.

On the evening he left, Opa prepared a farewell feast for Itabi. There was venison cooked in bear oil and garnished with wild parsley, and hot corn cakes served with conte jelly made from briar root and mixed with honey. The two ate well and said things to make one another smile. At the end of the meal, Opa took her son's face in her hands.

"It's time for you to shed your old skin, Itabi," she said softly. *"Your grandfather is so proud of you! He is at your side — we all are."* Opa hugged the boy and thought about not letting him go.

•

So when does the magic start, the boy asked himself impatiently.

He was on a trail that followed the steep bluffs along the great river. The main thing distracting him from his reverence for the Father of Waters were the mosquitos that feasted on his bare patches of skin. When he had said good-bye to Chucalissa three days ago, he'd set out with a sense of adventure. Now this vision quest was starting to feel more like an exile, he thought bitterly.

Where am I going?

The hot cakes his mother had prepared for him were almost all gone, and so too were the hickory nuts from outside their home. All Itabi had with him was a deerskin knapsack containing a water gourd, a pocket knife and his collection of agate stones he liked to find next to streams. He picked up a rock and flung it into the deep, coursing river below.

Now that Itabi thought about it, his situation had very few redeeming features. He was alone, hungry, and mostly defenseless, without anything resembling a plan. Who would want to be in his place? He was an outcast, a fugitive. *Ikanampolo.* He knew that his grandfather would've saved Fala and that everyone else knew it too.

As for me, I can't even speak properly.

Trudging forward, Itabi rounded a shady bend and found himself in front of a bursting shrub of huckleberries. Most of them were still red, but a small number of the berries had ripened to a healthy purple. He picked several handfuls and shoveled the fruit into his mouth, savoring the sweet juice trickling down his throat. Itabi looked at the huckleberry bush again.

While it was true that most of the berries weren't ready to eat, his attention had been drawn to the ones that were. If a person looked upon that bush ungratefully, the boy suddenly realized, they would never have given themselves a chance to taste the berries that *were* ripe.

Itabi decided that he must control his inner voice. He wasn't a fugitive or an unwanted child — he was on a vision quest to bring honor back to his people. All the stories are like this, Itabi thought to himself. People always had to overcome challenges that seemed impossible. Hadn't they doubted themselves too?

Those old storytellers, the boy mused, couldn't have imagined a time when their stories would go untold. They had assumed the sacred fire would never die. Itabi remembered how dry leaves sizzled in its flame, how the smell of burning pine once filled his nose so sweetly. Those were the moments he had learned of the heroes of *hacha hatak*.

The thrum and buzz of a nearby beehive made the boy feel drowsy. To his right was the dense forest, to his left the endless river snaking to the horizon. Something his mother had said came back to him. *"Read the signs,"* she'd urged him. *"They let you know you're headed in the right direction."* Itabi looked around him. It was hard to know which things to read.

I know, the boy thought to himself.

He took out the agate stones from his knapsack and arranged them in a triangle on the ground. Ever since he was young, Itabi played a game in which he repeated a word three times as his eyes followed the lines of the triangle. His grandmother had told him it was to help build confidence in his speech. Sometimes, when he went fast enough, he found that he could pronounce the words without a hitch.

Itabi thought of the word "blackbird" and resolved to use it for his game. This word was especially foreign to his lips and Itabi felt as though he had to fight to push the sounds into the air. He looked at the agate triangle at his feet and started to open his mouth. Before he could get the sound out, he was rudely interrupted.

"CAW! CAW!"

He looked up. There was a crow perched on the branch, black as night. The bird sounded its ear-splitting call one more time before taking off. The boy laughed out loud at the coincidence. Maybe, he thought, it was a sign to keep moving. He collected the stones and put them back in his knapsack. When Itabi looked up again, the crow was already gone.

The boy shrugged his shoulders, letting his eyes rove across the brown currents flowing into the distance. It seemed strange that, right as he was about to say its name, a black bird happened to make a noise above his head. It had to mean something, didn't it?

That was the sort of thing he heard the elders talk about in the tales of vision quests. In one story, a man had shot an owl with his arrow. When he went to retrieve the owl, it wasn't there. He turned around, only to see the figure of a man with the head of an owl standing before him. The owl spoke to the man for some time before sending him back to his village.

Just an old story, Itabi thought to himself. He stole a glance behind just to make sure, nonetheless.

•

He had been walking for several hours when he came to a fork in the trail. He could continue walking close to the river along the crest of the bluff, or he could plunge into the tunnel of the forest. There was less briar next to the river, but less clean water in the shaded forest trail. Itabi stood there for a moment, weighing his options.

He was startled out of his reverie by the sound of music behind him. *Who could it be?* Spinning around, Itabi saw an old man leaning against a tree with a flute pressed to his lips. No one had been there a second ago!

The old man broke off playing and held the flute out to Itabi. *"Have you ever tried?"* he asked with a smile.

The boy stood there looking at the flute-player, bewildered. He was unprepared for such an interaction. *"I don't k-know who you a-are —"*

"That's understandable," said the old man. *"Do you know who you are?"*

Itabi put his index finger on his chest and raised his eyebrows.

"Yes," the old man responded.

"Itabi, fr–from the Owl Clan."

"That's not what I asked." The old man smiled.

Itabi felt confused. He looked at the man for a moment. Long, silver locks of hair fell around his wrinkled face. He wore a sleeveless tunic with spiraling threads of turquoise sewn across the chest and a variety of medallions hung from his neck. Itabi had never seen such a beautiful flute. Natural oils enriched the deep color of the cedar and beads garlanded the instrument in a spiral.

The boy pointed at the flute in his hands. *"Did you m-m...did you make this?"*

"It was molded in the hands of Great Spirit, as we were too."

"So you're the artist."

"Isn't that saying the same thing?"

Itabi felt annoyed. What was this old man going on about? He couldn't make out what his words meant or what he was supposed to take from them.

"Do you kn–can you tell me where this path goes?"

This time the old man didn't respond, but only played a series of soft notes on his flute. His eyes never left the boy's face. Itabi turned away in exasperation and began walking towards the river. You never know what games people are playing, he thought to himself. It was better to keep moving. The old man's words, however, stopped the boy in his tracks.

"*Crown of the sky, father of waters, dancing daughter of four winds who brought the song of fire…*"

Open-mouthed, Itabi turned around and stared at the old man. Impossible! How could he know those words? Itabi had never seen this person before, and they were a several days' walk from Chucalissa. Then he realized…*a sign.* He sat quietly next to the flute-player, abandoning his desire to leave.

"*The flute teaches us to listen with our heart, Itabi. Every moment, the world finds a new way to speak to you. It is up to you to listen.*"

"*What c-c…which clan are you from, sir?*"

"*I have no clan, but all clans know me. Some call me Bearcloud. Chiefs call my name in times of need. I make myself of service.*"

"*And what do these chiefs w-want?*"

"*One thing, and one thing only: courage.*"

Itabi thought about this for a minute. *"How can you give them courage?"*

"By showing them their True Self."

The boy was quiet as he considered Bearcloud's words. Vaguely, he watched a white egret stalk its prey in the river shallows. It lifted one long leg at a time as it stepped through the dancing reflection of the sun.

"Does everyone have a True–a True Self?"

"Everyone, including you. Your True Self is connected to Great Spirit, and Great Spirit holds all things together in a perfect circle. Your True Self knows its destiny and calls it into being. Many people hide from their True Self; then its voice becomes mute."

"B-but why do they hide from it?"

"Perhaps for the same reason that you were ready to walk away a minute ago. They're afraid of what they might find."

The egret plunged its neck into the water and came up with something flashing between the spears of its beak. Two wings spread and it was soaring over the river and back into the whispering trees. Tomorrow it would come back and do the same.

"People are very skilled," the old man said, "at telling themselves The Story of Why-Not. The Story of Why-Not is driven by people's fear—fear of non-acceptance, fear of failure, fear of success. We reject our destiny when—"

"—w-when we give power to our fear?"

"I thought." Bearcloud laughed. "You didn't like when people finish each other's sentences."

The boy raised his eyebrows. He'd never met someone who seemed to know him so well. The wizened elder looked at him as though he were reading all of his thoughts and memories.

"If you are to walk this path, Itabi, are you willing to let go of the comfort of obeying your fears?"

"I-I...yes, I guess so?"

"No guessing! Speak so that your truth will be understood, and then be true to your word. You create your path with the words you speak. Do you understand me? Now, think of something you are willing to give up, then meet me here again tomorrow."

Itabi watched the old man recede into the forest. He scratched his head. He wondered when he would wake up to find himself back in his mother's lodge and this whole experience would be nothing but a passing daydream.

•

"I will tell you the wise men's biggest secret," Bearcloud said in a low voice.

"W–wait a moment," Itabi said in surprise, *"don't I need to be initiated first?"*

The old man waved off the boy's concern. *"It's simple: the problems people have are ones that they themselves create. This is what happens when people are trapped in their minds and fail to listen with their hearts. They solve one problem to create another."*

"How c–how could that be, sir? I didn't create my problem. M-m–I was born with this problem, can't you see?"

"No," Bearcloud replied. *"What your tongue does or doesn't do is not your problem, Itabi. The problem is your idea that your tongue can stop you from speaking."*

"It does stop me," the boy insisted.

"Yet your heart has much it wants to express."

"Y...well, yes."

"And is your tongue alone powerful enough to stop your heart from doing so?"

Itabi had never thought of it from that perspective. *"But w-what can I do?"*

The old man reached out his hand. *"What have you brought me?"*

The boy pulled the agate stones out from his knapsack and held them out. *"These–they're all I have."*

"Are they of value to you?"

"Yes, but w-why do I need to give them to you?"

"In giving up these stones, you show the Great Spirit that you are prepared to receive his wisdom. The path requires that you make clear decisions and sometimes that means parting with something you love."

The boy thought of his mother, the strawberry meadow, the sycamore tree. Had he given them up, or were they still with him in some way?

"Nothing is ever lost," Bearcloud said with a mysterious smile. His flute was leaned up against the bark of a tree. He picked it up and placed it in Itabi's hands. *"Try it."*

Hesitantly, the boy raised the instrument to his lips and began to blow into the mouthpiece. He pressed his finger against one hole, then another. The vibrations of the notes filled the air around him and made the hair on his neck stand on end. He closed his eyes and focused on the sound. It was as pure as water. Itabi opened his eyes and handed the flute back to the old man.

"What made that sound?" asked Bearcloud.

"Your flute, of course," said Itabi, amused.

"Resting in my hands now, does it make a sound?"

"N-Nobody is playing it."

"Exactly," smiled the old man. *"The flute-player no longer breathes into the flute."*

"I really liked those agate stones, you know," Itabi said with a sigh. He hadn't understood the old man's meaning.

Bearcloud let out a great laugh. He collected himself, then asked the boy for a drink from his gourd. Having taken a sip, he handed back the gourd and looked at Itabi for a spell. *"What is your pain?"* he finally asked.

"Th-That I am a failure to my clan."

There was a pause.

"Pain, struggle, and hardship," the old man remarked, *"are friends that tell you the secret of your gift. When you share your gift with the world, you have followed your Dream. Your pain is an invitation from the Great Spirit to do so."*

"But what is my gift?"

Bearcloud picked up his flute and indicated for Itabi to listen. Again, the vibrations of the notes surrounded Itabi, but this time there was a melody to captivate him. His ears followed its course in the same way his eyes had tracked the flight of the egret the day before. The boy's voice, to his own amazement, began to rise with the melody.

Crown of the sky

father of waters

dancing daughter

of four winds

who brought the song of fire

Our prayers rise

To bring down rain

And nourish the great mother

The song rose up between them and then, like a short rainfall, fell away. There was a special silence between the boy and the old man that felt as rich as the song itself. Itabi was stunned — he hadn't even stammered once! The words had flown from his lips as easily as the Miko's. It hadn't happened from thinking so much as feeling, he realized.

"Pain, struggle, and hardship," repeated Bearcloud, *"are friends that tell you the secret of your gift. When you share this gift, Itabi, the entire world will remember that it was waiting to receive it."*

"If I can sing...I can speak!"

"The Great Spirit plays his instrument quite well," the old man said with a wink. He took something from around his neck and put it in Itabi's hands. It was a beautiful emerald gemstone suspended on a necklace. The boy looked up wide-eyed.

"Y-You're giving this to me?"

"Think of it," nodded Bearcloud, *"as a way to remember who you are. If a person or thought causes you to forget, it will remind you."*

Itabi understood and put it on with a smile. *Where else have I seen an emerald necklace?* There were many things he wanted to ask, but the old man was suddenly preparing to leave. *"Where are you going?"*

"I follow my own path as you follow your own." He gave the boy a slight bow and turned toward the river, but then stopped and pointed at something. *"Look!"* A single firefly was floating over Bearcloud's head like a diamond.

"A good omen," he said with a nod of his head. *"Finding one's self isn't an easy thing, Itabi. But the magic begins when you trust yourself enough to take a chance."*

"Yakoke."

It was close to sunset and the sky was blushing pink and orange. Both watched for a moment as the firefly's light became indistinguishable from that of the sky. Itabi wondered if he'd ever see the old flute-player again.

•

Bearcloud chuckled as he climbed to the red ridge's summit. *"The chosen ones are always the same,"* he said out loud, *"naive and doubtful in the beginning and slow to catch flame, like a heap of wet logs."* His mind sifted through thousands of years of lived experience. When the flame caught, he reflected, the universe was transformed forever.

The old man placed a slab of basswood on the ground and sprinkled a handful of dried blossoms into the depression at its center. He then took a rod and, placing the end atop the tinder, slowly began rotating it between his palms. A wisp of smoke rose up to the violet-edged clouds. *"May the people of the Seven Clans,"* Bearcloud rasped, *"become the people of One Fire again."*

Flames sprung up at the mage's feet and danced with vigor. He muttered incantations under his breath and watched them slowly subside. The people were going cold with forgetfulness. Either their identity would fall apart or, soon, they were destined to take their place among the stars. The old man had witnessed both instances many, many times.

The future of the race depended on one little person's Dream. Bearcloud laughed in wonderment at the artfulness of the Creator. *"Forgive me, Great Spirit, for my audacity in presuming to understand your Work. Perhaps ages of service have granted me some passing moments of foolish pride..."*

From a distance, hunters could make out only an unknown glow on the hilltop.

•

The applause of the boy's imaginary audience wasn't loud enough. He cupped an ear towards the old oaks playfully then made a nimble spin. Ever since Itabi had parted ways with Bearcloud, he couldn't stop singing. He had sung at the top of his lungs all morning. Neither the river nor the sky seemed to mind all that much.

His voice was like a shiny new possession. *A gift.* The only other times he had used his voice for melody were during ceremonies in Chucalissa. His voice had half-heartedly joined the others, never fully distinguishing itself in that territory of harmonies. Itabi's attention had always drifted away from those moments. It hadn't occurred to him that, indeed, the flow of music freed his power to speak.

He saw that his voice could change colors whenever he wanted. It could go high and low, loud and soft, cheerful and somber. It could surge forward like the river or trickle softly like a creek. The voice had its own power. Itabi painted the air with every song he could remember, humming in places where he forgot the words.

The boy's past now seemed colorless in comparison. How is it that I never knew about this gift before, he thought to himself. Itabi recalled his litany of embarrassments and imagined how differently people would've thought of him had they heard him sing. Maybe Telulah would've returned my interest, he thought; maybe Fala would still be alive.

Part of him felt angry, as if he'd been cheated out of something. He knew he would never get that time back. He raised his hand to the emerald gemstone around his neck and closed his eyes. *All of the problems people have are ones that they themselves create.* Itabi felt a deep calm wash over him. None of those things matter now, he realized.

He made himself a promise: *"From now on, my thoughts and actions will only reflect the desire of my True Self,"* He said out loud.

There was no way to know what was going to happen next, the boy told himself. The only thing he could control was how much he trusted in himself — that was it. He couldn't control other people's thoughts and actions, so why pay them any mind? *When you share your gift, the entire world will remember that it was waiting to receive it.*

Itabi had a responsibility to his clan; his journey was theirs. Now, the boy thought to himself, I just need to understand what the journey *is*.

The nearest *talwa* was Chatelan, the chief town of the Bear Clan. Walking north along the river, Itabi calculated that he would reach Chatelan in a matter of days. He hadn't forgotten the prophecies of war in the council house. But Itabi also didn't know if what the warriors had said was true or not. Even if the Bear Clan had turned hostile towards his people, Itabi reasoned, perhaps there was hope for peace.

He committed himself to the Great Spirit and sent his voice back into the clouds.

•

I can't make a sound.

A shaft of sunlight fell on a herd of deer next to the creek. Their ears swiveled silently as they knelt to drink. Itabi, crouched in a grove of white oak nearby, was trying to load his bow without betraying his presence. His hunting experience had been limited to a handful of excursions with other boys in his clan where their performance had outpaced his.

The boy longed for a hardy meal of something beyond nuts, berries and herbs. When he found a bow washed up on the shores of the river, he'd decided to fashion his own arrows from sticks and scattered flakes of flint. This occupied more time than he'd expected. By the time Itabi finished, the summer sun was high and hot.

The deer hadn't suspected him. The boy had mumbled prayers to their spirits so that he could be granted permission to use their meat. Other hunters said that this was how humans kept their relationship with the animals of the forest. He took their word for it. Careful not to rustle a twig, Itabi moved into position, drawing the arrow back to his ear. *Patience...*

A movement on the other side of the creek interrupted his concentration. Itabi lowered his bow and looked on in curiosity. He saw what looked to be three antlered bucks approaching through the brush, but something in their gait struck the boy as peculiar. They weren't graceful; the trio kept stopping and starting, sometimes bumping into one another. What's wrong with them, Itabi wondered.

Suddenly, one of the bucks turned into a young man, standing and aiming an arrow. The herd scattered in a panic, grasping the deception too late. One arrow felled a doe with a shot in the throat; a din of whooping yells followed. Itabi watched in astonishment, still clutching his bow tightly.

"*A fine shot, Stone Foot,*" said one, removing his deerskin.

"*He hasn't had a clearer shot since he met the basket-weaver's sister,*" cried the other.

The three joined each other in laughter and began walking toward the fallen doe, their disguises shed on the ground behind them. Each wore two brown feathers in their long hair and wide grins on their faces. Itabi guessed they were around his age. He pressed himself against the tree, trying to determine his next move.

"*Say, Falling Fox,*" one of them said loudly, "*did you see someone behind that tree over there?*"

"*Why yes,*" Falling Fox replied, "*I think someone is hunting us for our antlers.*"

"*Shall we skin him alive, then?*"

"*W-wait, wait!*" Itabi stood up and emerged from the oak's shadow. "*I'm...please —*"

"*Please,*" shouted Stone Foot, "*His name is Please!*"

"*Please,*" the other two shouted in unison. "*Halito, Please!*"

"*B-but—*"

"*I am Stone Foot! We are the Bear Clan's Sun-Dancers, the greatest fire-stealers and storytellers of the Seven Clans. Join us —* "

"*Yes,*" broke in Light Cry, "*join us, Please, on our humble trek to Chatelan for —* "

"*The Green Corn Ceremony,*" Falling Fox yelled over the others, "*the moment we restore the sacred fire to the lodges of our people!*"

Itabi looked at the three of them in amazement, searching for the proper words to reply.

"*He's stunned,*" exclaimed Light Cry.

"*Awestruck,*" added Falling Fox.

"*Or puzzled,*" said Stone Foot. "Most would never guess such eloquence from a herd of deer!"

Itabi pointed at the fallen doe. "*Y-your kill...*"

"*Indeed,*" affirmed Falling Fox, taking on a pretense of sternness, "*we mustn't forget our kill. The Forest Elders are waiting!*"

The Sun-Dancers stooped over to collect the body of the doe, then lifted her as one.

"Are you coming, Please?"

"Yes, Please, where is your friend?"

"My friend?"

"You're Please, where is Yakoke?"

The three erupted in laughter and started walking through the light-dappled trees carrying the bloodied doe as best they could. Itabi slowly followed them. He was thoroughly confused by their behavior, but the words of one of them echoed in his ear: *The moment we restore the sacred fire to the lodges of our people.*

•

The air of the forest was dense, humid, and filled with a watchful personality. Itabi could sense the forest listening to the troupe of Sun-Dancers as they rollicked across its trails. His mother had forbidden him to retreat so far into the forest without good reason.

Up above his head the boy could hear the song of warblers, tanegers and meadowlarks as they prattled on like Falling Fox ahead of him. When they stopped for a breath, Itabi noticed how the green silence was deeper than any sound they could make.

There was a Spirit of The Forest, Itabi had heard, and a whole committee of spirit-beings that lived under its direction. Mostly they were indifferent to humans. Sometimes, it was reported, these spirits could be kind or ill-mannered depending on the person's heart.

Itabi tried to listen in the way Bearcloud had instructed. It was almost as though every creature's movement filled his ears, from the rustling of the bald eagle's wings to the squirming of the earthworm under mountains of dirt...

"Hey, Please!" The boy realized that all three of the Sun-Dancers had stopped to stare at him. One of them had the doe slung across their left shoulder. *"Tell us, where did you get that emerald stone?"*

Itabi opened his mouth to answer, but once again found himself interrupted. *"It isn't for us to pry,"* proclaimed Light Cry, *"he is a wanderer like us. A storied wanderer!"*

"Skilled in divination and dreamwork," ventured Falling Fox, turning to walk again. *"A fire-stealer fulfilling his destiny..."*

"That may be so," said Stone Foot. *"But I wonder how he knew?"*

"*How he knew what?*"

"*That we needed a fourth person to get through the Elders' Gate. It's too much of a coincidence!*"

"*Coincidences are like the smell of rain–they tell us that good favor is near.*"

"*Hey!*" Itabi finally broke in. "*W-I mean, who are the Elders?*"

The three stopped and gaped and Itabi, then exchanged a glance among each other. To Itabi's surprise, they all broke out laughing.

Light Cry turned around so that the dead doe's glassy eyes faced the other boys from his shoulder. "*'Who are the elders?'*" he mimicked. The laughter of Falling Fox and Stone Foot redoubled until they almost couldn't breathe. Itabi watched the outburst with some annoyance.

"*S-sounds to me like–like you don't know who they are,*" Itabi said suddenly.

The Sun-Dancers went quiet and stared at Itabi. "*It's a test,*" one of them said.

"*Hoke,*" said another, "*a test.*"

Itabi looked at their faces with amazement. These Sun-Dancers were sure a *strange* bunch, he thought to himself. He could hardly get a word in edgewise, but when he did, it seemed to cause quite a stir.

"We speak of the Forest Elders," said Stone Foot. *"Because we are Sun-Dancers, as I'm sure you know, the Elders don't allow us to pass through the forest without testing our Virtue. Our Virtue is our singing, our storytelling. We must recite a story of the Sun to gain passage over the cypress swamp–"*

"And leave an offering for the Forest Elders," added Light Cry, rolling his eyes to indicate the burden on his shoulder.

The Sun-Dancers began walking again in unison, resuming their airy chatter. The boy shrugged his shoulders and followed. He had to be patient, but too many questions crowded his mind to be answered at once.

•

The earthy stench of the swamp filled the boys' nostrils. They stood in a clearing with algae-covered water at their feet. Giant cypress trees rose out of the swamp's depths; their roots were like veins that fanned out in every direction. Each boy was surrounded by hundreds of cypress knees that looked like little wooden people standing in the water.

Light Cry placed the deer's body at the lip of the water and looked at others. They were all uncharacteristically quiet, Itabi noticed. *"It is time,"* Light Cry said, clearing his throat. The three Sun-Dancers breathed deeply and raised their hands in the air.

"Sh–should I–"

"If you can sing, then sing," said Stone Foot.

Itabi nodded. He kept hearing whispers behind him, but every time he looked around, all he saw were the clumps of moss draping the branches of hickory. *Are you willing to let go of the comfort of obeying your fear?* The boy was aware of the different thoughts in his mind; some spoke for Fear, others spoke for Doubt. Some even spoke for Hunger.

I must give this moment my full attention, Itabi thought to himself. Attention, his Miko had once said, contains the promise of right action. He swept all of his thoughts away and, like the Sun-Dancers, took a deep breath. Falling Fox was the first who lifted his voice to the Forest Elders.

At the dawn of the human world

All was dark, nothing to be seen.

Night stretched long and endless

All the world a dream.

Then woodpecker was heard to call

"The world's far side is crowned with light

Whereby creatures all rejoice

To escape the night"

Itabi recognized the melody but could only faintly remember the words. It had been so long since he'd met anyone who could still say them. Something odd, he realized, was appearing in the picture of the swamp in front of them. Itabi squinted. Dim halos of light were forming around the cypress knees in the water. Falling Fox became quiet and Light Cry began singing.

"Let me hide its light in my fur!"

Possum was sure he couldn't fail

And taking the Sun in his grasp

He burned his whole tail.

Next came Buzzard with sharp claws

And thinking his plan clever

He tried snatching the Sun

Then scorched his head feathers.

Each of the thousands of cypress knees in the water were now rimmed with light. They really *do* seem like little people, Itabi thought to himself. The boy had never seen anything like it before, nor could he understand it. He tried to remember to keep breathing.

As Stone Foot began the next verse, Itabi saw that the deer's body was slowly disappearing like a fine mist.

"I was made to bring you light"

said Grandmother Spider

Rolling clay in her big bowl

As they all eyed her.

Spider crawled towards the sun

Leaving a trail of clay behind.

She plucked pieces of light

Like grapes from a vine.

"This is it," the boys said excitedly, *"we're at the last part!"* The swamp seemed to glow like a late-summer night sky. Itabi wondered how the Forest Elders would help them cross over the water. More of the words, he realized, were coming back to him. Falling Fox stepped forward.

Holding the light she walked her trail

Returning from east to west.

Every place Grandmother passed

Her sun rays–

Falling Fox, on the verge of finishing the song, abruptly stopped short. His eyes darted back and forth in dismay. The others watched his face with growing panic—he'd forgotten. The song was left unfinished, hanging in the air. The Sun-Dancers knew the Forest Elders were impatient. Another voice suddenly began carrying the chant, like a lovely flash of silver.

Holding the light she walked her trail

Returning from east to west.

Every place Grandmother passed

Her sun rays did bless.

Spider chased darkness away

giving us the warmth of the Sun.

To this day she gives proof

In how her web is spun.

Itabi opened his eyes, his heart beating like a drum. The energy of his voice still coursed through his body. He felt as though he were floating off the ground. The boy's singing possessed its own power and the Forest Elders recognized it. Something, meanwhile, was happening in the water.

It started with a gurgle, then a plop. One of the cypress knees began to sail towards the center of the water in a trail of light. Another one moved, but to a different point yet in line with the first one. *"Watch this,"* the Sun-Dancers hollered.

Like shooting stars, thousands of cypress knees started arranging themselves in one long formation. They sped out and jostled for position with loud splashing sounds. Just like that, the wooden people had formed a bridge of light and now the boys could get to the other side.

The Sun-Dancers cheered and clapped Itabi on his shoulders. It was his first performance, one that he'd never forget. He understood the power of speech and how it could change the world around him. Itabi felt a huge relief. It was the kind of relief that comes from receiving an answer by living one's question.

"Come on!" cried Stone Foot. *"We have to be swift!"*

"Stay on the tips of your toes," called Light Cry, *"and don't lose your balance!"*

Each boy waited five seconds for the other to get a head start, then began hopping from one cypress knee to the next. Itabi saw how easy it was and mimicked the Sun-Dancers' technique. He kept his eyes half-closed to avoid the glare. Ahead of him, Falling Fox, Stone Foot, and Light Cry were hooting with joy as they scaled the bridge, hopping like frogs.

Itabi looked up. He wasn't sure, but he caught a glimpse of something on the opposite bank. It looked like the same doe that the Sun-Dancers had slain. The animal watched the boys, fire dancing in its eyes. Itabi felt like it was looking straight at him. Then, in the same instant, it was gone. The Forest Elders had accepted their song.

•

The fire they'd made was meager, but the Sun-Dancers' spirits were high. Night had fallen and the forest was filled with the sound of the tree-frogs' mating calls. The sound was like the beating of the drum, Itabi mused, because it was so constant that you forgot it was there.

Four squirrels were turning on a wooden spit, thanks to Falling Fox's skill of tempting them with a rattle. Itabi's stomach growled as the smell of burning meat filled his nose. *What would happen if we lost the sacred fire?* Itabi looked at the smiling faces of the Sun-Dancers and dismissed the thought. He needed to stay positive, like them.

It was a funny thing that, even though they shared his gift, the Sun-Dancers seemed to have a different personality from Itabi. They liked to talk and talk and talk. They talked so much, Itabi thought to himself, that they hardly ever seemed to listen.

Nonetheless, they always knew what to say. What they said, however, wasn't always important.

They were going to Chatelan, too. Even if they were a little crazy, they were also like guides on his vision quest. There were many, many questions Itabi wanted to ask them. More than anything, though, he needed them to understand his story. They had to realize that they had to stop interrup—

"Hey Please, take this knife. You stare into the fire so much that it might get scared and run away!"

"Itabi. M-my name is...Itabi."

"But you told us your name was Please," laughed Stone Foot.

"No, I didn't. You d...you didn't let me finish my sentence."

"Yeah, stop interrupting him, Stone Foot," joked Light Cry.

"You too, Light Cry. All of you. I c-can't speak the same as you Sun-Dancers. My words don't flow like...they don't flow like yours."

None of them said anything as Falling Fox passed around the freshly cooked meat. Each began to cut at the flesh with sharpened flint knives.

"Where are you from, Itabi?"

"Yes, and how did you get the name 'Itabi'?"

"You're —"

"Interrupting again? Sorry..." Falling Fox smiled at Itabi sheepishly.

"I come from the Owl Clan, and I have left to fulfill my name...I have l-left to find how I can heal my people."

"Itabi from the Owl Clan!"

"He howls, with the wings of an owl—"

"Stone Foot, what happened to that woman from the Owl Clan? The one —"

"Enough," barked Stone Foot. The others stifled laughs.

"I-I...maybe you can tell me something," interjected Itabi. *"Our warriors think that the Bear Clan has cursed us. But you...you are from the Bear Clan, and I s-see that your fire is low too..."*

"*All of us are cursed,*" said Light Cry. "*It is not just one tribe or another. All seven clans have lost the sacred fire. All seven clans fight the same enemy–the enemy of forgetting…*"

"*Our fate is the same,*" said Stone Foot.

"*Yes, Itabi, our fate is the same,*" repeated Falling Fox. "*That is why we travel to our native Chatelan for the Green Corn Ceremony. Our feet will dance, our voices will sing, our words will tell the old stories–*"

"*We are the fire-stealers,*" said Stone Foot.

"*The w-what?*" Itabi searched their faces, each inflamed with the dance of the light and crisscrossed with long shadows.

"*The fire-stealers. It's like the song about Grandmother Spider. 'She plucked pieces of light like grapes from a vine.' We became the People of One Fire when our ancestors were gifted the light of the Sun. Now we must get it back–without the fire we are nothing.*"

There was a lull in the conversation as the four boys hungrily chewed at their hunks of meat. Squirrel wasn't Itabi's favorite, but he'd never been so thankful for a meal. Friendship fed him too. The din of the tree-frogs rose and fell around them in the darkness.

"*You are a fire-stealer too, Itabi,*" said Light Cry finally.

"*I can sing, I know that now. But what can I do with...with my voice?*"

"*Come with us to Chatelan,*" replied Stone Foot. "*Join us in the Green Corn Ceremony. You will be welcomed there. It is a good town, there is much trade. The Miko's hope is strong for the sacred fire to return —*"

"*It is rumored,*" said Falling Fox in a lowered voice, "*that the priests will journey to the Emerald Mound. Yes, the holy Emerald Mound! They say there is magic there. Our people have always known it to be a place of destiny.*"

"*How can w-we get there?*" asked Itabi immediately.

"*You can't just go there,*" laughed Falling Fox, "*you have to get permission from —*"

"*The elders, the priests, the Miko!*" said Light Cry in an exaggerated tone.

"*You can go,*" said Stone Foot, "*only if they know that the Great Spirit wants you to...*"

"*It is my calling to go where the Great Spirit asks,*" blurted Itabi. The remark caught even Itabi by surprise.

His tongue had delivered the words smoothly, like a piece of music.

"In that case," replied Falling Fox, *"you will be blessed with a woman who can fly you to the moon."*

Itabi joined the others in laughter; soon they broke into wild singing as the fire slowly dwindled back into the void of the night.

●

The boy's thoughts were swarming in his head like the pigeons so great so great in numbers that, on some afternoons, they blocked out the sky. These were new, exotic thoughts that he'd never experienced before. He felt both excited and confused about what his excitement meant. The vision of the Emerald Mound now commanded all of his attention.

I must get there, Itabi thought to himself, it's my place of destiny. He finally knew the joy of having a Dream—and the anxiety too. The boy felt like a different person. In only ten days, his whole life had changed, and he saw the world from a new perspective.

Ih-Ih-Ih. He thought of the people in Chucalissa, everyone he'd grown up with. Some of them would never travel this far, he reflected. The boy saw that his experiences had changed him from who he was before, but that his journey was only beginning. He ran his fingers along Bearcloud's emerald stone, thinking of its place in his vision quest. *Itabi.*

Itabi had never felt like he mattered to anyone. Everyone else around him had a reason for *being*; they all seemed to have something they were good at. As Opa's troubled son, Itabi always felt like a misshapen knife, of no use to his clan. Ever since the Miko had sent him away, everything had become the total opposite.

He saw for the first time that he *did* matter, everyone did, because everyone had a gift to share; if only they could allow themselves to do so.

Hope was hard to come by, the boy reflected. Ever since the night of the fateful thunderstorm, no one in the Owl Clan had possessed the courage to hope. The sacred fire had shrunk, ceremonial dances had fallen into disarray; the knowledge of plants and medicines had vanished and so too had the people's power to dream.

Why had the sacred fire been taken away from them? Perhaps, the boy thought, the people had lost the connection with their True Self. That's what Bearcloud would say, anyway. *Without the fire we are nothing.* It was easy to turn away from hope, but Itabi's confidence had grown so quickly that hope was the only thing he allowed himself to feel.

His friends had called themselves the fire-stealers. Itabi understood the importance of Grandmother Spider and the old stories of plucking fire from the Sun. Still, it seemed to the boy that they needed to *remake* the fire rather than steal it. The sacred fire was a part of who his people were—it connected them to the dreams of the land, the sky, the Great Spirit.

The people thought that fighting each other would lead them out of darkness. Even now, Itabi knew, the warriors of his clan were sharpening their weapons and taking less food in preparation. How wrong they all were! It was just as his mother had said at the council meeting. It was easy for people to give in to fear and suspicion when they hadn't found their True Self.

If I can reach the Emerald Mound, the boy thought, I can help remake the sacred fire. He hadn't planned on meeting Bearcloud or the Sun-Dancers, nor could he have imagined it, but there they were. Now he was following his new friends to join the Green Corn Dance in Chatelan. Something would happen there; Itabi could feel it.

Ih-Ih-Ih. Nobody knew why his mother named him after the howling of the wolves. Then again, Itabi had never known that he could cast his voice like a silver rope into the sky. He thought of his grandmother, how she told the story of the pawprints next to the creek. A powerful chill ran through Itabi's body like a shock of lightning.

Everything that was happening seemed like it was meant to be. His name was easier to say now; he took pride in it. Itabi was shedding *ikanumpolo* like old snakeskin. When he arrived in Chatelan, the boy resolved, no one would doubt why he had this name— a name of destiny. *Ih-tah-bee.*

•

A cypress canoe sought shelter from the gathering rain clouds under the draping boughs of a weeping willow. Kallo's paddle cut through the water without a sound. The canoe drifted through the sweeping curtains of green as the first big raindrops stung the young man's broad shoulders. *"Where are those half-wits,"* he said out loud to no one in particular.

Kallo was someone impatient by nature. It had less to do with being punctual and more to do with the excellence which he liked to picture himself representing. He had a big idea of who he was; so big that there was little room in his thoughts for anyone else.

His grandfather was an important man in Chatelan. That was why the young man's neck shone with pearl and strings of imported seashells. A deafening clap of thunder split the sky in two; raindrops were puncturing the river's surface with numberless needle-points. He shook his head, pulling his cloak of bark and feathers around his shoulders.

His impatience was growing, as usual, with the other Sun-Dancers. Kallo spat into the water with disdain. They'd agreed to meet him the night before. Their own indolence, Kallo supposed, had prevented them from doing so. Everyone knew he was the greatest dancer in Chatelan–was there any doubt that he held that title for all the Seven Clans?

It was Kallo who had instructed the Sun-Dancers what to sing for the Forest Elders. *Could they have forgotten the song?* The young man shuddered at the thought. Soon the town would begin to stir with preparations for the Green Corn Ceremony, the biggest celebration of the year. He was sure they could illuminate the town-square with the spirit of fire as they did in the old days.

Kallo would be dressed magnificently for the fire-dances in his bird costume, his face streaked with paint and arms hung with trailing feathers. How handsome he would appear to all the spectators! He would wink at his secret admirers as though making a pact with each of them. His feet would soar to the beat of the drums as Chatelan roared as one.

"*Yes,*" he commented to the weeping willow, "*this is my moment! It's no secret why we've lost the sacred fire, is it? We lacked excellence as a people, and so the Creator had the idea to squeeze us out. Grandfather lost his speech because his tongue lost its power. When I bring the sacred fire back, everyone will witness my superiority!*"

The old willow swayed with indifference in the howling rain. Kallo leaned back in his canoe, hands clasped behind his head. He felt pleased when he was the center of attention. This summer's Green Corn Ceremony would see many dignitaries and tribal leaders who didn't normally make the trek to Chatelan. They would be there to witness and Kallo was sure that he would become a moment that would live on in history.

Kallo was born as the Sun was being swallowed by a beast in the sky. The members of his clan were going to great lengths to save the Sun—they ran in this direction and that, whooping at the top of their lungs and making a clatter on their drums to scare off the beast. The darkness was heavy and absolute. Giving birth to her little one in the sky's long shadow, the mother felt that the child must possess unearthly power. Hence the name, *Kallo*.

None of the elders could remember a more complete eclipse of the Sun; nor could they remember a child being born during such an event. When the Sun made its return the next day, the Bear Clan rejoiced. Kallo was the symbol of their triumph over the elements. Surely, he was destined for greatness, they thought. His grandfather was a grand priest of the sacred fire, after all.

Kallo's birth was seen as a good omen for Chatelan's growing fortunes. Built on the rich floodplains of the river, Chatelan was a bustling center of trade and craftsmanship. It imported gray-blue quartz from the western mountains and sea-shells from the southern coastline. The people of Chatelan were known for their refinement in clothing and carried themselves proudly.

Kallo and the Sun-Dancers channeled this flamboyance into their performances. They dressed lavishly in conch shells, face paint, bright mantles and long eagle feathers. The style of their fire-dance was flashy and high-flying, filled with moves that required rare brilliance. The children crowded around, cheering them with *oohs* and *ahhs*.

At the last New Moon Festival, the lead Sun-Dancer had sat with the elders in the great council lodge for the first time. This was where the priests and medicine men would discuss the mysteries of their knowledge around the sacred fire. Kallo was taken in as one of their pupils. He listened raptly as they spoke about the Emerald Mound and his chest swelled with pride.

The rain was still pouring in sheets around the weeping willow and its canoe. Kallo fingered the sea-shells around his neck with restlessness, envisioning his future fame and success. The willow's billowing green curtains were an empty canvas for the pictures in his mind.

He saw that the fire-dance lifted his feet into the clouds and brought him eye-level with the Sun.

The rhythm of the drum filled the heavens as he reached out his hands...descending, his clan would hail him as an Elder from Above, his shoulders dressed in white buckskin. If they ever escaped this eclipse, it would be because of *him*.

I don't need anyone to like me, Kallo suddenly thought to himself, I just need them to respect me as the hero I am. *That is what really matters.*

He knew that he had peers in the Seven Clans who also wanted the same thing he did. This made Kallo suspicious of strangers from other towns. He knew that Falling Fox, Stone Foot and Light Cry had in all likelihood met a fourth person in order to pass through the gate of the Forest Elders. Who could it be,

Kallo wondered. The person could be from any one of the Seven Clans...

If he were to join the Sun-Dancers to Chatelan, Kallo resolved, he'd have to learn his place.

•

"Who is Kallo?"

Itabi and the Sun-Dancers were huddled under a makeshift awning of hide propped up by tall stakes dug into the ground. The rain had been relentless for over an hour with no signs of stopping. The boy had managed to ask his friends how they planned to reach Chatelan.

"Remember," started Light Cry, *"how we said you're the fourth person in our group? He's the other fourth person."*

Itabi scratched his head in confusion.

"There can't be two 'fourth persons'," said Stone Foot, rolling his eyes. *"There's only one fourth person, and then a fifth person."*

"That may be so," replied Light Cry, *"but seeing as either one could have served as the fourth person for the*

purposes of passing through the gate, both Itabi and Kallo can technically be referred to as the 'fourth person', you see?"

"Yeah," interjected Falling Fox ironically, *"I see that you're a raving lunatic!"* Light Cry playfully shoved the other two, sparking a brief squirmish.

"Hale!"

The Sun-Dancers stopped and looked at Itabi with faint grins on their faces. *"Th-that tells me nothing about who Kallo is!"*

"He's a Sun-Dancer," said Falling Fox plainly.

"No, he's the Sun-Dancer!" exclaimed Light Cry, raising one finger in the air.

"The Sun-Dancer?"

"Look, Itabi," said Stone Foot finally, *"Kallo is our leader; he's like a little Miko. When people come to see us dance, they're really coming to see him dance. He's very popular in Chatelan."*

"Kallo dances with wings on his feet," added Falling Fox.

Itabi thought about this as the currents of rain crashed through the canopy and formed little rivulets running through the soil. They told him how Kallo had agreed to wait for them at a specific point along the river where the forest opened up.

"Does he t-talk as much as you guys?" The Sun-Dancers all laughed in unison at the boy's genuine inquiry.

"There's something you should know," ventured Stone Foot. *"You can't always take what Kallo says personally. Sometimes he says things—"*

"He's just not always the easiest person to know," shrugged Light Cry.

"Why is that?" Itabi looked from face to face with both eagerness and anxiety.

"Sometimes, when you're the best at something, you might look down on other people a little bit. Kallo is sort of like that. He's not a bad guy, just—"

"A little conceited," said Light Cry, finishing Stone Foot's thought.

The boy nodded; his forehead creased in thought. He could certainly understand the type of person the Sun-Dancers were talking about. The Owl Clan had several personalities like that, most of them young hunters. They strutted around town, boasting of their adventures with a twinkle of pride in their eyes. Everyone had to know they were the best.

Itabi had always looked at those other boys with a mixture of envy and resentment. That was back in Chucalissa when he hadn't understood his gift. Now he looked upon this kind of personality with new eyes. Itabi thought it strange that someone like Kallo would use their gift to make others feel low about themselves. *Isn't a gift supposed to bring joy?*

"Come now, Please," cried Falling Fox, clapping Itabi on his back, *"why so glum?"*

"I got it," laughed Light Cry, *"let's give him some drums and release his voice into the sky..."*

The Sun-Dancers started creating a rhythm with their mouths. Itabi grinned; he'd never seen such spontaneous creativity before. He began swaying back and forth, releasing all of his worries. A chant issued from his lips, finally, that made them all forget they were huddled together in a rainstorm.

●

They found Kallo on the banks of the river the next morning, bathing in sunlight. His canoe was moored near him in the shallows. The blue sky was as clear as a mountain spring; the great river itself burst forward in sparkling renewal.

"Finally," yelled Kallo to the Sun-Dancers, *"what took you so long, huh?"*

"We were busy telling the Forest Elders of your accomplishments," yelled back Falling Fox with a look of mischief.

"If that were so," Kallo laughed, *"you would be stuck in the forest until the snakes themselves wrapped around your limbs!"*

Itabi got his first look at the charismatic performer. He was taller than Itabi and the other Sun-Dancers, with broader shoulders and a pronounced jawline. His hair draped over his shoulders in two pigtails and he wore fringed buckskin leggings. Kallo's movements radiated supreme confidence.

He fixed his eyes on Itabi as the group approached, squinting in scrutiny. *"He is from the Owl Clan,"* Kallo said, addressing the Sun-Dancers as if Itabi weren't there. *"I can tell by the way his moccasins meet the ground!"*

"Kallo, we met this young man by pure chance," said Stone Foot, *"he is one of us. If not for him, we wouldn't have crossed the gate —"*

"His voice shines like crystal from the western mountains," exclaimed Light Cry.

Kallo studied the boy's face. *"What's your name?"* he demanded.

"Itabi — from the Owl Clan."

"The Owl Clan," sneered Kallo, looking at the others. He walked up to the boys and began circling them as he talked. *"There are many things we need in Chatelan. There are many things we need in the Bear Clan. A singer is not one of them — especially not one from the Owl Clan. How do we know this Itabi isn't working against our people, confusing our senses with his sweet serenades?"*

"Sweet serenades? Kallo, you're being —"

"I want to hear from the outsider!"

Itabi mustered all of the courage he had and looked Kallo squarely in the eyes. *"My grandfather w... was also a medicine man. He lost his power to speak, like yours. I-I can't speak very well. But my voice is magic, and... all of our people need magic now."*

Kallo arched his eyebrows in surprise. *"You're Shikoba's son, then?"* Itabi nodded his head.

"Kallo," Light Cry said, bursting with indignation, *"the Green Corn Ceremony is here. We don't have a singer like him. With all of our talent put together, we can persuade the elders and priests to take us to the Emerald Mound. Can't you see? It's destiny."*

"Where is that emerald necklace from?" Kallo asked with a surly expression.

"Bearcloud," replied Itabi. He saw no reason to be dishonest.

The Sun-Dancers all exchanged looks of surprise. *"They say Bearcloud is a legend of our people, nothing more,"* said Stone Foot. *"You're telling us you met Bearcloud and he gave you that necklace?"*

"Y-yes, he did."

Kallo snorted and turned around as if to walk away, then faced Itabi again.

"I'm hungry — if you can catch a fish for my breakfast, you may join us and become a Sun-Dancer. If not, we will leave you here to fend for yourself. Do we have a deal?"

Itabi looked to the others, but they only shrugged and looked at the ground. He could see how Kallo's presence changed the equation of things. The boy glanced at the flowing waters beyond where they stood. The great river was as ancient as time but unceasingly youthful in its energy.

Every young boy was taught to be as swift as a salamander in its currents.

"I will do it." His heart was racing in his chest.

The boy saw that if he walked through the brush to the left of the sandy bank, he would reach an outcropping of rocks which jutted out over the water. He recalled a technique he'd seen his peers perform outside Chucalissa on numerous occasions. *The magic begins when you trust yourself enough to take a chance.* Itabi sighed and began making his way to the rocks.

It occurred to him to commune with the fish as the hunters did with the spirits of the deer before making a kill. It should work the same way, Itabi thought to himself. He murmured a prayer to the aquatic spirits as he stepped through ferns and clumps of tall reeds. *They are one with the Great Spirit too.*

When the boy reached the rocks at the lip of the water, he stripped off his leggings and wrapped his breechcloth around his right palm so that part of it dangled like a string. The red color would serve as a bait for the fish — or so he hoped. He caught a glimpse of the emerald necklace flashing in his reflection on the water's surface. *Here we go.*

Itabi lowered one leg into the river and then slid down the rock with a splash. The warm freshwater enveloped his limbs and sent a tingle up his spine. He felt Kallo and the Sun-Dancers watching him, just as he had felt the elders' gaze when he had knelt at Fala's side. There was no turning back now. He plunged in headfirst and opened his eyes underwater...

Everything was blurry, murky, green. The first thing Itabi noticed was how the sun rays formed columns of light that cut through the water's depths.

As his vision adjusted, he saw that he didn't need to swim so far down to reach the river's bottom. Catfish loved hiding beneath the rock beds. He dove downward, the strip of red breechcloth drifting in the current.

Besides a fleeing turtle, the river seemed empty. Itabi was thinking of how much longer he could hold his breath. Another 20 heartbeats. He waved the strip of breechcloth in front of an opening in the rock bed, and turned to swim upwards. There was a flash in the corner of his eye.

Itabi couldn't believe it — out of nowhere, two giant catfish were trailing the bait in his hand with long whiskers swaying in the water. They were almost at the surface. With one swift, upward motion, the boy pinned the two fish together between his palms and rocketed them out of the water. Both sailed through the air and landed flopping on the rocks.

Falling Fox was the closest to the scene and began hooting in glee. The others rushed around; to their amazement, more catfish were being ejected from the water. *Two, four, six*...it was as though the sky was raining fish on the banks of the river. The performers from Chatelan had never seen anything like it. They fell upon the catfish, chanting snatches of different songs in excitement.

"Never mind a fire-stealer, Itabi, you're a fish-stealer!"

Kallo took in the scene and narrowed his eyes. Who was this stammering boy, he wondered. There seemed to be something different about this Itabi; the others treated him like he was *na lakonchi,* a savior. Now he was walking towards Kallo, soaking wet with a brave grin on his face.

"Will that be enough f-for your breakfast?"

Kallo curled his lips and looked away. *"So, are you some kind of expert fisherman or something?"*

"No, they...today they just came to me."

"I see. Your tricks will only get you so far, Itabi. If you come with us, we have to know we can trust you. You are no better than any of us. Understand?"

"I-I am true to my word," replied Itabi, *"my word is my truth."*

"Twelve fish, twelve fish!" hollered Light Cry before Kallo could answer. *"That's enough to get us to Chatelan..."*

The boy smiled to himself. He'd only just realized that he and Kallo were standing beneath a sycamore tree.

•

Part 2

"Thief! Thief! There is a thief inside the walls of Chatelan!"

The people milling about in the town square took a collective gasp. From the entrance, a pair of young men ran to notify the Miko. The accused man did not attempt to protest or escape; instead, he stood in front of the palisades, his head hung in shame.

The town-crier repeated the crime for all to hear, "any man who takes *tanchi* from the fields on the eve of the Ceremony is in contempt of the Great Sun. He must be purified of his sins before we can pay tribute to the sacred fire! There is a thief, a thief—"

It just so happened that as this drama was unfolding, Itabi and the Sun-Dancers finally made their arrival. It was the first time that the boy from Chucalissa had laid eyes on the tall palisades of Chatelan. Two bear sculptures towered and flanked the eastern entrance. Itabi's eyes, however, trained on the guilty man.

He was a middle-aged man with a small mohawk crowning his otherwise shaven head. He wore nothing but a breechcloth. The man was clearly humiliated—he stared down at the ground, clenching and unclenching his fists. Next to his feet was a knapsack from which a small hill of kernels had spilled.

Without much delay, the second chief and his contingent appeared at the entrance. The twin Miko, as he was known, wore a plume of eagle feathers in his hair and bright pearls in his ears. He looked at the spilt corn at the man's feet and then sternly at his face.

"Explain yourself, nakni tashka. What can we understand from this?"

"My family suffers, Miko," the old warrior replied. *"The Sky Elders have taken from my wife her skill in engraving seashells and in doing so they have also taken from us our sustenance, our well-being. What Ceremony is there if we don't have any ears of corn for our children?"*

"You admit to committing thievery then," the twin Miko replied. *"How can we expect grace from the Sky Elders if we show no virtue in hardship? You must cleanse yourself immediately, brother, so that your sin doesn't linger here among the People of One Fire."*

The man was silent. He stared at the ground in embarrassment and fury. There was nothing to do but accept his punishment in front of the gathered onlookers. An older man with long white hair stepped out of the twin Miko's contingent. In one hand he held a large conch shell, in the other the razor-edged jaw of a garfish. Itabi's eyes widened at the scene.

The old warrior held out his arm. The sharp teeth of the garfish jaw were pressed into his skin and yanked downward. Four trails of blood, red as garnet stone, ran down his arm. The old warrior's chest heaved and his breath growled. The white-haired man then handed him the conch shell. It was filled with some liquid. The old warrior drank the liquid and immediately began to gag, eyes bulging.

When the man scampered out of sight, no one went to stop him.

"In such manner," yelled the town-crier, *"will any person be treated for taking or eating even a single kernel of tanchi on the eve of the Ceremony! Such has it been for as long as our ancestors have walked these lands, and so will it always be! Yamohmahe alhpesa!"*

Itabi stood there, stunned. He knew the ceremonial code but had never seen it enforced. What a strange way to enter a new place, he thought to himself. The boy sympathized with the old warrior and his troubles. If the men in Chucalissa only knew! As far as Itabi could see, things were no different in Chatelan. He grimaced as he heard the old warrior vomiting around the far corner of the palisades.

"Don't get any ideas, Itabi," said Falling Fox, grinning. He patted Itabi's shoulder. "You don't want to drink that stuff, trust me."

"Yes," joined in Light Cry, laughing. "Welcome to Chatelan!"

"The rainbows will come out tomorrow," added Stone Foot with a wry smile.

It was then that the town-crier spotted their troupe for the first time. *"Kallo and his Sun-Dancers have* returned to Chatelan! Not only that, they've brought another young man with them – another dancer for the Ceremony, we can be sure!"

The townspeople who had gathered to witness the punishment quickly forgot everything about it. They were excited to greet the ceremonial dancers and to find out who the young man was. Itabi found himself confronted by a flock of strange faces, their expressions all burning with the same question. The boy remembered that Chatelan was to be the birthplace of his True Self, a new beginning for his life.

Just as Itabi was about to make an introduction, Kallo stepped in and spoke for him. *"This boy's name is Itabi. He is our new Sun-Dancer for the Green Corn Ceremony. Let it be known that he comes from the Owl Clan –* " The onlookers, prone to gossip, let out a gasp. *" – yes, but he will be under my strict tutelage! If anyone has a problem with Itabi, he can come to me."*

The boy was seething. Who was Kallo to assert himself over Itabi? Impulsively, he raised his fist in the air. *"I am here to restore the sacred fire!"*

Falling Fox raised a whooping cry that spread among the townspeople like a wave of hope. Kallo whirled from one foot to the other in a continuous circle, perfectly balanced. Everyone cheered his brilliance.

Itabi could see why the people of Chatelan loved Kallo. He commanded the people's attention with the charisma in his body and the confidence in his words. He knew how to use his smile like a sunrise breaking over the horizon. He always left the people wanting more. He was a natural performer who excelled in creating moments that everyone remembered.

The canoe ride, however, had been filled with tension. Kallo had sulked for much of the trip, refusing to share in the mirth of others. When he did speak, it seemed to Itabi that Kallo only said things to make others feel low or unworthy. He wanted Itabi to know that he could never truly be a Sun-Dancer. That wasn't what had angered the boy the most, though.

One night as the group was reclining on the riverbank gazing at the stars, Kallo had asked Itabi a question.

"Do you know why our clans are two instead of one?"

Stone Foot groaned. *"Kallo, must we get into this?"*

"How boring," agreed Light Cry, *"to speak of such things now."*

"W-What does he mean?" Itabi asked.

"As I expected," Kallo said with arrogance. *"You were never told the full story. You know about the pole, don't you? How it was to stand crooked or straight?"*

The boy nodded, unsure in what direction Kallo was taking the conversation.

"Yes, well only half the people thought that it was straight. Those are your people, the Owl Clan. The other half saw that the pole was still leaning north. They kept journeying till they came to what is now Chatelan. They were patient enough to keep traveling, and they were rewarded with a superior land. Those are my people, the Bear Clan."

There was silence; Kallo's words hung in the air like the stench of foul meat. The other Sun-Dancers felt uncomfortable. Itabi, for the first time, felt a rage inside of him. These words were meant to sting him, and they had.

"So...so what?"

"So when you come to Chatelan, know your place. You are lucky to number yourself among the Bear Clan...but you will never be one of us."

Since then, Light Cry had told him a thousand times to not pay attention to what Kallo had said. Itabi knew that Light Cry was wise in telling him this, but Kallo's dark words weighed on his heart nonetheless. He was on a journey in the name of his clan, but everything his journey had taught him so far was that his destiny went beyond the Owl Clan. Kallo seemed to know this, too.

Why is he speaking with the ignorance of the warriors back home?

The boy snapped back to the moment. Chatelan was no longer a story, but his new reality. Taneger birds warbled in the trees and children played in the town square. They told him to let go of the past and place his moccasins squarely in the present.

•

There were too many new impressions for the boy to handle at once. He walked across the town square with Light Cry as though in a daze. Chatelan seemed to spin in many colors of excitement; the dusk ushered in the biggest ceremony of the year.

The plaza was filled with the joy of long-awaited arrivals. Some came with deer meat, hickory nuts and squash, while others simply brought themselves. There were visitors from neighboring Bear Clan towns; some others were ambassadors from the Eagle and Snake clans. Many were already dressed in their special, ceremonial dresses of long, rattlesnake-pattern skirts and ribboned tunics.

Itabi could hear the faint sound of drums rumbling through the air. It sounded like the very heartbeat of Chatelan. The river of faces streaming around him almost made the boy dizzy. This town was at once familiar and unlike anything he'd ever seen. It was bigger than Chucalissa; more vibrant. There was a beauty in Chatelan's strangeness. Itabi longed to become one with its dancing movements.

"Come on, come on!" Light Cry urged, shaking the newcomer by the arm. "You will see everything soon, young dreamer. My uncle is waiting on us..."

The Sun-Dancer led Itabi away from the town square towards a settlement of clay cottages with roofs of thatched straw. Light Cry had told the boy little about his uncle Ikbi, besides the fact that he was one of the few potters left who were still able to reproduce the traditional designs. He had also said that if Itabi wanted to have a roof over his head, he had to hope Ikbi would make him an offer.

Presently, they came to a large cottage whose facade was lined with a collage of earthenware. There were pots, sculptures, plates, and vessels of different shapes. Many of the tobacco pipes were made in the form of animals. Their faces were so vivid that Itabi expected the snakes to hiss and the wolf cubs to whimper.

"The spirit of tobacco will bring them to life," said a voice behind them.

"Halito halito, uncle!" Light Cry exclaimed, laughing from the surprise.

Ikbi smiled graciously and embraced his nephew. Itabi could see that he was a quiet, humble man devoted to his work. When people have inner strength, he reflected, they put those around them at ease. Ikbi nodded at his nephew's new friend and invited the boys inside. There was a low fire burning in Ikbi's cottage that was echoed in every home across Chatelan.

Itabi and Light Cry stepped inside and sat down on a bench lined with mink furs. Ikbi filled two clay cups of water for his guests. Itabi found himself mesmerized by Ikbi's hands—they seemed to make the act of pouring water into a steady, nimble dance. They were the hands of an artist who never lost his connection with the earth.

Ikbi politely asked about his nephew's trip, allowing the exuberant young man space to describe some of his adventures. Itabi noticed that, as Light Cry carried on in his dramatic way, there were moments in which Ikbi cast an inquiring eye onto Itabi's face, as though he was searching for something there. The conversation soon turned to the Ceremony.

"In the old times," remarked Ikbi, *"the renewed flame was lit in every hut on the second day of the Ceremony. It has been said that soon the sacred fire will wane to such an extent that the women will only be able to light a handful of huts with its flame. What does it mean, the people ask? Shall we all live together under one roof, like bees in a hive? The elders are unsure of what to do."*

"It has also been said," Light Cry replied, *"that perhaps the Great Spirit wishes for us to separate into*

smaller tribes. What if Chatelan has grown too large and decadent? Some think it is wise that we scatter ourselves across the land like leaves in the wind..."

Ikbi turned to Itabi and addressed him for the first time, his eyes sparkling with intelligence. "I have listened to my nephew tell of your success at the cypress swamp. Tell me, Itabi, what was it that you felt when you sang your song?"

Itabi thought for a moment. *"In...it was inspiration."*

The potter leaned back against the wall with his eyes cast down into the fire. The boy thought about saying more but decided against it. He could see that Ikbi was careful and deliberate in his ways—a far cry from the temperament of his nephew. Light Cry shifted restlessly next to him. Ikbi rose from his seat, finally, and lifted a tall staff that was leaning on the other side of the hut.

"I made this," Ikbi said, *"for the People of One Fire."*

At the head of the staff were the sculpted faces of the totem animals for each clan: bear, owl, eagle, snake, wolf, raccoon, deer. *"All you see, Itabi, is an object. That's all we see. But this object was created from a spark of inspiration. Can you feel it?"*

Itabi nodded. He had never seen such an exquisite staff in all his life.

"The Great Spirit gave four of our people each a staff, our legends say. He taught them how to make fire with their staffs by turning one end on the ground. When each of the four men saw that their staffs were burning, they joined them together, creating the One Fire in the center. This is the sacred fire that will burn forever, gifted to our people from the Creator...

Itabi, there are things that people let die. One is wisdom, another is hope, and another, memory. We cannot let our memory die – if it's lost, then everything is lost. That is my inspiration in what I do." Ikbi gestured toward the animal faces on the head of the staff. *"Our memory must live on."*

"Uncle," Light Cry jumped in, *"Itabi wants to reach the Emerald Mound. He's said so since we first met him in the forest. He is a dreamer, a holhpokunna. When Kallo made him jump in the river, he caught more fish than – "*

"I have heard you, nephew. The one you speak of is here with us. Itabi, what is it that you wish to do here in Chatelan?"

You create your path with the words that you speak. The boy had repeated Bearcloud's words in his mind over and over again the night before they reached town. *My words are powerful, even if they aren't spoken perfectly.*

"I-I wish to go to the Emerald Mound; I wish to use *my gift to heal our clans. That is what my grandfather wants. My voice — it is the same as your staff. It's an instrument... an instrument of memory.*"

"*And may this voice, this instrument be held to the fire for all to see, as I have shown you my handiwork?*"

"*But Uncle —* "

"*It's OK, Light Cry,*" Itabi said, "*i-it's only fair.*"

The Sun-Dancer raised his eyebrows. "*Do you want me to do that drumming thing, or —* "

"*No need,*" chuckled Itabi. Feeling the presence of Bearcloud next to him, he knew the melody he wanted to use to color the air's canvas.

Crown of the sky

father of waters

dancing daughter

of four winds

who brought the song of fire

...

Itabi sang it twice, filling Ikbi's cup until it was full. The potter was almost moved to tears — he smiled at the boy and nodded his head in appreciation. *"You are welcome to stay here, holhpokunna, you are most welcome. I only ask that you help fetch water and mind the fire...perhaps nourish this lonely man with a song on occasion..."*

"I am grateful, Uncle Ikbi. And will you s...will you show me how it is you remember the old ways?"

Ikbi smiled at the boy's earnestness. *"As the Great Spirit decrees it, young man."*

Light Cry jumped up like a rabbit. *"Now you've really arrived in Chatelan!"* He was beaming from ear to ear, already on fire from the energy of the Ceremony.

Soon, Itabi knew, Ikbi's nephew would dance till sunrise. It was a time of new beginnings.

•

"We drink this elixir to refresh our bodies," whispered the first voice, *"and flush out everything eaten in the old season. Thus we have done at the beginning of every new harvest. We renew ourselves to renew the world...you know what our teacher has said — "*

"I know the tradition," snapped a second voice, *"but what you are suggesting is completely impractical! We cannot brew the passa elixir if we are unable to remember its contents, can't you see? If we use the wrong snakeroot, what will happen when the people drink it?"*

"I've told you already — this white snakeroot must be the ingredient used in passa. When the Miko's nephew returned to Chatelan with a snakebite on his rear, our teacher healed it within a day!"

"I will return with the same reply: any snakeroot can do the same, but that doesn't mean it is the one used in our Ceremony since the birth of the Sun, understand? We want to purge our bodies without the risk of poison. If the snakeroot is bad, you'll wish you only had a snakebite on your rear!"

"I will try it," whispered the first voice defiantly.

"Are you mad?" the incredulous voice shot back. *"The wrong snakeroot can kill you!"*

"Then let my body provide us the answer."

Itabi had been lying awake when he overheard the voices outside Ikbi's hut. He guessed from the door's gray sliver of light that it was dawn. Hearing what the first voice aimed to do, the boy shot up and opened the door. Two young men stared back at him with startled expressions. Both wore white feathers in their hair and rich copper around their necks; one was holding a horse conch-shell filled to its brim.

"Wait! You mustn't, you...j-just stop!"

Both young men stared at the strange boy speechlessly.

"He's right, it's-it's not the right plant," Itabi pressed on. *"The People of One Fire, we use the blue s-snakeroot for the passa elixir, not...not the white one."*

"On whose authority is this told to us?"

The boy told them his name and his clan. *"I am the grandson of Shikoba and tomorrow night I will perform as a Sun-Dancer,"* he added with confidence.

"And why should we believe you, Itabi? You say the flowers should be blue and not white, when in reality it could be the opposite. Even now, one of our fellow apprentices is drunk from a vine we thought to be an ingredient, and he thinks that every tree is trying to catch him."

The second man chuckled and shook his head, digging one foot into the dirt.

"I-I can still remember some things." Itabi replied, *"You want to make passa? Take the blue snakeroot and mix it with...with tobacco, cedar, and red berries. For the w...the White Drink, you need the cassena plant."*

The boy didn't know how he knew these things. When he was at Fala's side, the chant had alighted on his tongue from nowhere. It was as though all the old rituals the clans had forgotten were hiding within him, waiting to be spoken somehow.

The second man indicated the conch-shell containing the white snakeroot brew. *"So what will happen if my friend here decides to drink this?"*

"He would fall very ill and...get chased by all the trees."

The man laughed, shooting his friend a look of derision. *"If he's right, you may owe someone from the Owl Clan your life!"*

The first man shrugged his shoulders. *"Let us go first to the elder council and hear their thoughts on the matter. May we tell them your name, Itabi? The fasting begins tomorrow and decisions must be made soon."*

The boy nodded. The three paused to admire the Harvest Sun as it broke over the horizon to grace the land with its morning rays. Chatelan sat silently in the new light, but soon the town square would teem with activity — people would clean out their huts and rid themselves of all the things they no longer needed.

"I am Two White Feathers," said the first man.

"And I am Wolf's Friend," said the other.

"We will see about your blue snakeroot elixir," added Two White Feathers.

"Y-You should probably empty that out," Itabi said, raising his chin at the horse conch-shell.

"I don't know," replied Wolf's Friend with a smile, *"my friend still might want to try some."*

"Just empty it out," Two White Feathers scowled. Itabi stifled a laugh. The horse conch-shell glittered as Wolf's Friend turned it upside-down, releasing the

snakeroot back into the earth. The young men walked back towards the council lodge. Soon, the Sun would rise high over the great river.

•

"He wears an emerald necklace, does he not?"

"Yes, Miko," replied Wolf's Friend, *"the boy from the Owl Clan. He speaks with a stammer –"*

"Yet it's been said that his voice is superior to anything we've heard in Chatelan."

Wolf's Friend nodded but gave no reply. The young man was seated meekly on the ground next to the fire of the council lodge. The Miko of Chatelan, Musholatubih, and the mute high priest Shanafila sat in their honorary seats positioned above the fire. Wolf's Friend stoked the flames with a long stick, hoping in vain to revive its power.

Shanafila was so named for his special relationship with hawks—he was never seen without one perched on his shoulder. There were many who wished to gain this skill, but it required years of initiation within the mysteries of the clan. Shanafila was limited to communicating with the Miko and Wolf's Friend through a series of hand gestures.

"There cannot be many like him left among the Seven Clans," mused the Miko. "Who else can recite the ingredients of passa as though the clouds never eclipsed our Sun? For one harvest, at least, this boy has restored one of our sacred traditions."

The door opened, blinding the occupants for a moment, and a sturdy figure stepped inside. It was Kallo. He paid respects to his grandfather and the Miko before taking a seat next to Wolf's Friend. Shanafila's blue hawk stretched its wings but remained perched on the medicine man's shoulder.

Musholatubih gave Wolf's Friend an encouraging nod. Turning to Kallo, the young man gave an account of Itabi and the ceremonial elixir. Once they had gathered blue snakeroot, tobacco, cedar and red berries, Shanafila's pupils tested the mixture on a person in Chatelan.

This was a man who, according to the Ceremony's tradition, had just been pardoned of past crimes. He was eager to help Wolf's Friend and Two White Feathers if it meant atoning for his behavior. Within minutes, the *passa* took effect — the man purged himself outside of the town square.

"He has reported no symptoms of illness," Wolf's Friend concluded, "*unlike the poor man who was caught stealing tanchi a day ago and has yet to show signs of recovery.*"

Shanafila began signing furiously with his hands. Kallo had never made an effort to learn how to understand his grandfather, so he relied on Wolf's Friend as an interpreter. "*He says,*" Wolf's Friend began, "*that this boy Itabi has given the Bear Clan something we've lost for years. We want to know more about him. What have you learned since he became a Sun-Dancer?*"

Kallo's face cast downward, burning with indignation. This Green Corn Ceremony was to be his moment of glory and no one else's. Now his grandfather and the chief were treating Itabi like a savior, a *na lakonchi,* just as the Sun-Dancers had done when the boy had been lucky enough to catch some fish. *Impossible!*

He looked up with a cunning expression. "*There is no doubt this Itabi has some talent. It's a favor to the Owl Clan that he has made such a reputation for himself. Still, I would counsel some caution. We know very little about him and if I'm being honest, I'm afraid he's shown signs of dishonesty –* "

Shanafila cut his grandson off with a series of hand signals. *"He asks,"* Wolf's Friend explained, *"what have you seen that leads you to say this?"*

"Grandfather," Kallo continued, *"when we were canoeing up the great river together, our conversation turned to the elixirs of our people. We talked about how sad it was that no one could recall the herbal preparations of the old days. When he asked me to guess the ingredients, one of the plants I mentioned was blue snakeroot — "*

"Kallo," interrupted Musholatubih in a severe tone, *"you mean to say that you are to receive credit for our rediscovery of passa, not this boy from the Owl Clan?"*

"Miko, you misunderstand me," Kallo replied tactfully, *"I don't wish to receive credit for anything that happened by sheer luck. I only tell you this for the fact that the boy is not without ambition. As you taught me, grandfather, a man led by ambition is without conscience. But there is also another thing, which I hesitate to mention..."*

The Sun-Dancer took a dramatic pause, as if what he had to say next pained him greatly. *"His stammering, I believe, is an act. It's something he uses to win attention. I started to suspect this when we were journeying up the river together, because I noticed the impediment would only occur when everyone was listening. In private conversation, his speech was perfectly normal."*

The Miko narrowed his eyes in silence. Next to him, Shanafila's hands were in a flurry of motion. *"Those are very serious accusations,"* translated Wolf's Friend. *"Can we be sure that your words have nothing to do with your own ambitions, Kallo?"*

"Grandfather," the young man burst out, *"this boy told us that he met Bearcloud himself in the wilderness! Really, he did! How are we to trust someone who blinds our eyes with such tall tales?"*

The Miko raised his eyebrows. Fluent in Shanafila's sign language, he turned to the medicine man and began a silent conversation. Kallo's eyes darted back and forth between the two leaders. The Miko was resplendent in his mantle of white buckskin, a tuft of snow-white feathers on his crown. On Shanafila's shoulder, the blue hawk preened itself and stretched its talons.

Finally, Musholatubih turned once more to the pair of young men seated next to the fire. *"If this boy Itabi says that Bearcloud has crossed his path, then that is a big story indeed. Neither of us have ever seen this man, and many of us think Bearcloud only to be a myth of our people. We have, however, heard stories in the past from those who swore they met this holy person in the woods.*

Kallo, we have listened to your misgivings about Itabi. We will keep a close eye on him as the Ceremony unfolds. However, we will continue with the resumption of our passa ritual, as we have gone without it for too many harvests. Be it luck or otherwise, we must admit that this boy has done the Bear Clan a great service. I'm sure you will agree."

The Sun-Dancer started to say something, but the Miko held up his hand for silence. *"We expect to hear his voice tomorrow night at the stomp dance. Wolf's Friend, prepare enough passa for all of the men in Chatelan to drink tomorrow. We are all ripe for rebirth. Yamohmahe alhpesa!"*

As Wolf's Friend followed Kallo out of the lodge, something the Sun-Dancer had said rang in his ears: *a man led by ambition is without conscience.* He shook his head and went to find Two White Feathers.

•

Itabi shook off a yawn. The boy's dreams were like the white smoke of the town's fires, disappearing into the sky. His new life in Chatelan seemed so much like a dream that he had little energy to remember the ones he had while he slept. One of them drifted back into his memory, however.

He was on a path and just ahead of him was Fala—running, running. She kept looking back at him and calling something out. He tried to run faster to get within earshot. Finally, Fala's voice carried to his ear, *"keep running, you mustn't stop...keep running!"* Looking up, he saw that the Sun was slowly being eclipsed. When he looked at Fala again, all he could see was her emerald necklace in the wind.

The boy instinctively touched the smooth stone at his throat. How was it that Bearcloud had given him the very emerald necklace that Fala was so famous for wearing? *It will help you remember who you are.* Itabi remembered how Fala's eyes cut at him in the dream and a chill went up his neck. He had a strange feeling that her spirit was guiding him in some way.

Itabi thought of his journey through the forest and the promise he had made with his True Self after meeting Bearcloud. His voice had sounded so lonesome there among the whispering trees. Here he was now, amid the Green Corn Ceremony and its cascade of sensations. Soon, that same voice would be leading Chatelan in a stomp dance, a sacred tribute to the Creator.

Fala was right; all he needed to do was press onward. There were times the boy wanted to give into amazement, to look on in wonder at his magical experiences. But he had the innate understanding that now wasn't the time for amazement—it could come later. His mission was to reach the Emerald Mound and remake the sacred fire.

In doing so, he prayed that Chatelan would remember that it was waiting to receive his gift.

"Itabi, Itabi!" The boy turned around—it was Ikbi, carrying an armload of old clay pots. *"Can you take these to the town square for me? I have so many old things to get rid of—we all do, I suppose."*

The boy gathered the pots from Ikbi, reciprocating his gentle smile. He had been wandering between the people's lodges aimlessly, still feeling himself to be somewhat on the outside of the new town's pulsing rhythm. It was nice to have something to do. *"Join me for a meal soon, holhpokunna,"* the potter called after him.

Itabi headed for the center of Chatelan with his armload of pots. Every man, woman and child seemed to be engaged in the same chore — some carried threadbare clothes and worn-out baskets, others had utensils and trampled bearskins. All of it was to be burned that day in the town square, swept aside for the new things of the new year.

He let the scene wash over him, not attaching to any one perception but rather taking everything in at once. The boy saw the finery of the people's ceremonial clothing and listened how the language took form on their tongues. Children rushed past him in shrieking laughter; pieces of conversation caught his ear.

There was a comfort in knowing that nobody knew him for who he had been before. Itabi had only dreamed of that kind of freedom — now it bloomed in his hands.

The boy reached the center of the square. He found himself in front of a mounting heap of all the things the people no longer had use for. Casting Ikbi's pots into the pile, Itabi paused to watch as the town set itself free from its old belongings. He noticed pieces of jewelry gleaming here and there among the dusty shawls and snapped woodwork.

He finally understood the wisdom of the ritual. When people surround themselves with things, Itabi reflected, they become worried about losing them. Opa had always told him that a man who only keeps what he needs is happier than a man who only thinks of what he wants. He wished with all his heart that his mother was in Chatelan with him. Itabi smiled at what she might have said.

Something caught his attention that caused him to double take. *How could that be?* A stack of beautiful paintings, all on buckskin attached to wooden frames, suddenly clattered into the heap. Itabi's eyes quickly moved to the hand that threw them. There stood a young girl, not older than 12 or 13 years. Her short hair framed a gaze that seemed both resolute and uncertain.

"Hey," Itabi said, stepping towards the girl, *"c-can I ask why do you throw these...these paintings away?"*

The girl looked at him for a moment, startled. Itabi felt embarrassed. *"It's just...those paintings are so pretty. Are they yours?"* Her expression relaxed and she turned her gaze back in their direction.

"They were," she said in a small voice, *"but now they belong to no one."*

The boy considered this for a moment, unsure of how to respond. He felt as though he should help her in some way. *"Are you sure y-you don't want me to...I can – "*

"No," the girl said, raising her voice, *"they must burn! They're only imitations of what they want to be. Let them burn in what is left of the sacred fire!"*

"What they want to be? Forgive me, I-I'm not a painter..."

The girl let out a sigh that seemed more like that of an adult than a child. She wore a fringed deerskin dress with red beads and long white feathers attached to her earrings. *"It's a lot to explain,"* she replied glancing at Itabi again. *"Do you know anything about art?"*

"No, just singing," Itabi replied.

"Singing, huh?" The girl gave it some thought. *"If you ever sang off-key, would you want to hear it over and over again?"*

"N-no, of course not," the boy said, laughing.

"So maybe you can understand why I'm throwing those pictures to the fire."

"But — those pictures are beautiful!"

"If you could see what I wanted them to be," the girl explained, "you might say different."

Itabi looked once more at the paintings, sitting there in the filth like deserted treasure. He was stunned. *How could they be more beautiful?*

She giggled at Itabi's bewilderment. "*They call me Running Hair,*" she said, "*but that was before my haircut! I think I'll need a new name soon…*"

As they walked away from the busy square, Itabi found himself listening in fascination to Running Hair's story.

•

"*When I was 9, I had a dream that I was watching a sunset. This sunset had the wildest colors I could imagine. I thought the sky was on fire. There were purples, yellows, reds, pinks. I had never seen colors so alive. In the dream, I heard a voice tell me that one day, I would paint a sunset just like it.*

From that day on, my only interest has been to paint the sunset of my dream. I have tried and tried — you wouldn't believe how many times! Almost every evening, I climb up to the same place next to the river. I even named it myself: Sunset Bluff. I sit on a big rock and watch the sky change colors. Then I start painting.

Hale! My paintbrush has nothing of the skill of our Sky Elders. Sometimes I come close, oh so close...but then my timing is wrong, or often I don't have the colors that the sky does. I only have juice from berries, blues from little rocks I find, mixed with fish eggs. It is nothing compared to what the Great Spirit uses, you see?

Sometimes I wish I never had that dream, Itabi. My parents say I'm too young to be so serious all the time. The other girls my age play and play. If I hadn't seen that Dream-Sunset, maybe I would play with them too. Hale! It is my path and I believe what the voice told me. One day, I will paint my Dream-Sunset and our people will see something they've never seen before!"

Itabi found himself touched by Running Hair's fierce determination. She was younger than he was, and yet already her passions were inflamed by a Dream. The boy marveled at how much of Running Hair's story seemed to mirror his own. They were both committed to something bigger, even when that commitment caused others to misunderstand them.

As the girl talked about the colors of the sunset, Itabi couldn't help but notice all of the colors around them. There were the deep indigos and oranges of women's skirts, the delicate turquoise of aquamarine earrings, the streaks of face-paint that were as ochre as the vases Ikbi made, along with feathers and beads that ranged from white to red.

"Have you...have you ever tried to get colors here in Chatelan?" Itabi asked suddenly.

Running Hair looked at him with a mixture of surprise and amusement. *"Here in Chatelan? What a strange thing to say!"*

"Well," the boy replied, *"w-why not? Look at all of these beautiful things people are...are wearing. I look at them and see all the colors of the sunset. Isn't that what you need?"*

"Of course, it is," the young girl laughed, tossing her hair. *"But why would anyone want to help me? They use their dyes for clothing and many other things. Who wants to waste that on some little girl?"*

Itabi thought about it for a moment, then was struck by an idea. *"Y-your paintings!"*

"Uh-huh...what about them?"

"Why don't you tr...why don't you trade your paintings to the merchants for the colors t-they have?"

"Trade my..." Running Hair pondered the boy's idea with a knitted brow, then suddenly looked at him in wonder. *"Mother told me that some clans up the river trade many a good things for enchanted works of art! Do you think...?"*

"I do," smiled Itabi. *"If I were a merchant here in Chatelan, I-I know I would buy some."*

Running Hair wasn't listening; her eyes were glazed over in dizzy calculation. *"...I could get indigo, a lot more indigo, maybe some blue and white, and yellow would be so wonderful..."* She brought her hands together and giggled in excitement. *"Then I'll know the secret of the sunset!"*

The boy laughed politely and looked to the sky. White clouds lazily draped the day's gaping blueness. Running Hair, studying his face, realized that she had never seen Itabi before. He was young and his face was kind but with the perceptiveness of a child. She could sense there was something different about him.

"It must be hard for you to talk with people sometimes," she said softly.

The boy's eyes widened with surprise. Few people outside of his family, if any, had ever spoken to him directly about his stammering. For a brief moment, Running Hair's remark flooded him with the old sense of shame and self-loathing. Itabi took a deep breath and exhaled. *My thoughts will only reflect my True Self.*

"Sometimes," he answered with a smile, *"but when they know me for...for who I am, it doesn't matter. I follow my own Dream, like you. Maybe I can't speak l-l-like the Miko. Fine, but my gift...my gift speaks for me."*

"You've already found your colors, then," nodded Running Hair.

Itabi chuckled, admiring the young girl's analogy. *"Ever s-since I've started this vision quest, people have recognized my power. Before, they only saw my weakness. The only thing that's changed is...is my thinking."*

"Are you sure you're on a vision quest, though?" Running Hair asked, her head cocked to one side. *"I think those only happen in the forest – "*

Their conversation was interrupted by a shrieking sound directly over their heads. Looking up, Itabi saw what looked to be the silhouette of a giant hawk against the brightness of the sky. It seemed to be circling the spot where he stood, getting closer and closer. *What is that bird doing?*

He wanted to say something to Running Hair, but she wasn't there anymore. She must've taken off in fright, the boy thought to himself. Squinting his eyes upward again, Itabi realized that the hawk had vanished too. He looked around — the bird of prey was already a little dot over the river. Itabi shrugged his shoulders and turned homeward.

"Hey, Please, we've been trying to find you everywhere!"

It was the Sun-Dancers minus Kallo. Itabi grinned, relieved to see familiar faces. Falling Fox, face painted, stepped forward and threw a square of corn cake in Itabi's direction. *"The last snack of the old harvest, holhpokunna."* Itabi devoured it hungrily; he'd barely eaten all morning. *"Soon the fast will begin!"*

"Come on," urged Stone Foot, *"we still need to rehearse the stomp dance all together. It's your first one as a singer, right?"*

The four Sun-Dancers departed together in good spirits, teasing and clapping one another on the shoulder. Itabi didn't notice until later that a single blue feather had, somehow, become lodged in his necklace.

•

"Abstaining from food, my friend, also implies abstaining from talking about food," said Wolf's Friend, rolling his eyes.

"Every year," replied Two White Feathers, *"the only thing that saves me from dying of hunger is imagining myself to already be at the Ceremony feast. As I sit there, giddy with expectation, the plates begin to arrive. Roasted turkey, hot corn cakes, steaming bowls of hominy grits, bear ribs, mounds of red jelly — "*

"Hey, enough! I can see it all so clearly and taste it so vividly on my tongue that I feel guilty of having broken our fast, and I may as well be subject to punishment at the hands of Shanafila before the dance begins this eve!"

Two White Feathers grinned in response. They were sitting on the white sand of the ceremonial grounds, stoking a new flame that was now even lower than it had been on the first day of the Green

Corn Ceremony. Both were covered from head to toe in white clay, giving them a ghostly appearance.

"You should've seen him this morning at dawn," Wolf's Friend continued, *"when we put out the last of the old fires, so fearful was he that the sacred fire wouldn't rekindle...the holy man was practically trembling!"*

"It doesn't seem to have much long..." Two White Feathers trailed off, dreading where the thought might take them. *"Still, the blue snakeroot elixir was a success today, was it not?"*

"Through the mercy of the Great Spirit, it was! Did you see the expressions on our warriors' faces as they drank it?"

"I did, they looked as though they had been stung by a hornet..."

Wolf's Friend snickered, shaking his head. *"That's not what I meant. Yes, the drink is strong and bitter, but the feeling of honor for having taken part in a ritual of our ancestors for the first time — that is a sweet, sweet thing."*

"The word is passing around that this boy from the Owl Clan is the one who has restored our passa tradition. The Sky Elders have looked favorably upon us, they say. It is a good omen."

Wolf's Friend remained quiet, coaxing the flame with his long staff.

"Do you not agree?" pressed Two White Feathers, observing his friend's apprehension.

"My only fear is what Kallo will do in reprisal, that is all." He went on to explain the scene in the council lodge on the previous morning, of how Kallo went out of his way to portray Itabi as an imposter. *"His words dripped with jealousy such that, after serving my duty as an interpreter, I saw it fit to wash my hands."*

Two White Feathers gave this some thought, his clay-smeared face wreathed in smoke. *"Do you sense that Itabi is trustworthy?"*

"I do," said Wolf's Friend thoughtfully, *"although it is hard to guess the intentions of a stranger. I trust that his actions will show us who he is. As for Kallo, his character is no mystery to us. He will do anything to make sure the Sun shines brightest on him."*

"Akat," the other young man agreed.

Both fell silent. All around them, the town was surging in anticipation of the stomp dance that would soon inflame the ceremonial grounds. Brush-topped arbors had been erected at each corner of the square, and dignitaries from the Snake Clan and Deer Clan had already begun to take their seats. Their ears were eager for a new, triumphant voice.

Wolf's Friend, unsure of how to feel, decided to change the conversation.

•

DUN-duh-duh-duh-DUN-duh-duh-duh! The drums were pounding outside the council lodge, slowly picking up their pace. Itabi's freshly painted face shone with anxious sweat. He had long since tuned out the talk of the others around him, feeling himself more and more tethered to the Ceremony's pulsing rhythm.

What if the great river overflowed, Itabi thought to himself, and the entire town was buried under currents of water, sparing me of having to lead the people in song? Grimacing, he shook off his mind's nervous ideas and turned his senses once again to the sound of the drums, to the energy of his voice that lay coiled in his chest like a serpent waiting to rise.

The moment had arrived and it had found a version of Itabi that Chucalissa wouldn't have known. Here he was in the full regalia of a performer – face and bare chest illuminated with red and white paint, shoulders hung with a mantle of eagle feathers, neck encircled with copper ornaments covering the emerald on his throat. In his right hand was a tall, feathered staff.

The Miko's tobacco smoke filled Itabi's nostrils. When the Sun-Dancers had sat down with the Chatelan chief hours ago, he'd passed around Itabi's *passa* elixir in a wooden cup, along with a long tobacco pipe. Musholatubih had smoked first, taking long draws before puffing clouds in the direction of the Great Spirit above, and then in each of the four directions.

"You have honored the Bear Clan in granting us our old memories," the great chief had said, raising the cup in Itabi's direction. Itabi felt both dizzy and elated. The Miko was known for being a man of few words – a mere sentence was understood to bear a lifetime of fortune. His tobacco leaves, Itabi found, were no less potent.

DUN...DUN...DUN! A sudden variation in the drumming returned Itabi's attention to the ceremony. Musholatubih stood alone in the square of white sand, arms raised above his headdress. It was time to issue the sacred copper plates and staffs to the warriors before the stomp dance.

"Ah, mah! We are the People of One Fire, given life by the Master of Breath, the One in the Sky that gives us light, whom we now honor in the holy Busk ceremony of the summer harvest. The People of One Fire are today threatened by darkness, hunger, and we now look to our dancers, the bearers of light, memory, and tradition, to guide us through the shadows of misfortune..."

The Sun-Dancers had filled Itabi's ears with a similar message the day before. *"You mustn't forget,"* Light Cry had insisted, *"what we talked about around the fire after passing through the gates of the Forest Elders! Do you remember?"*

"Yes...I remember."

"It is far easier to forget," added Falling Fox, *"then it is to remember. Every year, our clans have carried feathered staffs and the ancient copper plates so that we can remember our story and avoid forgetting. Now, the elders believe, it may no longer be enough."*

"We are the fire-stealers, the bringers of knowledge, the grandsons of Grandmother Spider, Itabi!" Light Cry continued. *"It is your voice that will reawaken Chatelan and shower it with the glory of the Sun. You must prepare a new song for the stomp dance..."*

"What k-kind of song? How will I know what to say?"

"First, you must — "

"Imagine," Falling Fox broke in, *"the sound of the turtle-shell rattlers on the women's ankles as we dance around the fire, how your voice will sound against their constant beat, which is the pulse of the earth herself."*

"Yes," nodded Stone Foot, *"and imagine that you are speaking to the Great Spirit in prayer, and that the voice of the people responding to your words is the voice of the Great Spirit himself, answering all of our prayers."*

"And imagine," said Light Cry excitedly, *"that your voice is the match that will reinvigorate the sacred fire, just as the howling of the wolves prickles our ears and reminds us of the moonlight's grace..."*

The boy had thought about this deeply. *How can I make a song that reminds us of something we already know?* He kept circling back to the dream with Fala and his afternoon with Running Hair, and somewhere in his mind a chant had begun to take form. *"They will listen,"* his mother had said to him, *"they will listen — "*

"Itabi!" With a start, the boy found himself looking into Light Cry's striped face. *"Now is not the time to reenact how Stone Foot got his name. Hale! Our time is now!"*

Looking past the charged-up Sun-Dancer, Itabi saw a row of faces all staring back at him. The warriors held the copper plates, richly embossed with pictures of legend, and the women stood in their dresses of burning colors with turtle-shells tied to their ankles. They watched as Itabi appeared from the council lodge and walked between their ranks.

The boy who was the butt of jokes in Chucalissa, whose name everyone ridiculed, now stood in the heart of Chatelan as a *na lakonchi* — he was too carried away in the moment, however, to notice that something was attached to his feathered staff which hadn't been before. The stomp dance was already turning around the fire like a great wheel.

•

Way hey ya hey ya!

You a hey you ay!

A hey ya a hey ya!

Way hey ya hey ya!

You a hey you ay!

A hey ya a hey ya!

The sound of stomping feet, rattling turtle-shells and Itabi's own swooping cries mingled with the odor of smoke and sweat as dusk descended on the rivertown. Hundreds watched in reverence as the Sun-Dancers guided Chatelan through one of its oldest rituals. The motion of the dance hypnotized the eye, following a spiral that ended only after many had surrendered to sleep.

What started as a small contingent of dancers, singers and warriors now swelled to full capacity as children and their grandparents alike rushed to join, matching their steps to those already in the circle.

It was natural to watch the catlike Kallo as he leapt, whirled, spun, and flipped around the fire without losing rhythm. The voice of the lead singer, though, had stirred the people's fervor.

Some were startled to realize that the new sound wasn't from an instrument. The voice was unlike anything they could remember — it seemed to take on the qualities of the great river itself, washing over the floodplains in waves. The boy's voice rose above the town square; it expanded itself to every corner of the palisades without losing its richness. The people suddenly felt as though the very stars were within reach.

The pace and volume of the drums picked up, straining to meet the intensity of the lead singer's chant. Dignitaries from the Snake Clan leaned over to exchange whispers with one another. More amazing than the voice itself was its miraculous ability to stir recollections in the minds of everyone present. Itabi's voice was like a mirror in which Chatelan saw itself again for the first time.

While Kallo's expression was unchanging, the other Sun-Dancers were delirious as they circled the fire, their ululating cries by far the loudest in the dance.

Itabi had come up with a song that, while very unique, was in a familiar call-and-response form. As he sang his questions, every person was able to join in on the answers, all their voices together becoming the voice of the Creator.

O Great Spirit, we children of the earth

Cry for your brilliance in the caves

Of despair, will you not hear our cries?

Yes, dear Son, for I always have.

O Great Spirit, if your fires are

Eclipsed, how may we reflect your

Light when we smile to our beloved?

I will see, my dear Son, to your happiness.

O Great Spirit, will you help us

Remember all the ways our hands

And words once worshipped you?

Yes, dear Son, for I am all around you.

O Great Spirit, will not the joy

Of the great river wane as the

Land is overtaken in darkness?

All things, dear Son, take life in my grace.

O Great Spirit, is it not enough

To paint our faces with the colors

You paint the sky at sundown?

In the sky, dear Son, is the token of my love.

Round and round the circle went as Itabi shed his verses, casting his questions across plumes of smoke and having them answered again and again. The people had achieved a forgotten ecstasy, yet it was still no match for what Itabi was feeling. He seemed to hover above the dance like a cloud, beyond the borders of time, somewhere close to Fala.

Itabi's voice now sang on its own. The rest of him merely watched how the warriors' copper plates gleamed in the fire's light. A voice reached his mind: *Don't lose heart now, Itabi.* What could it mean, he wondered. The drums were like thunderclaps and his song flashed like lightning. *Don't lose heart now.*

Someone's yelling brought the boy back to himself. Something was happening; the dance had been disrupted. Itabi's voice trailed off into thin air like the fumes of the sputtering fire. *"Look! He's an imposter, see for yourself!"* People looked around with raised eyebrows and blank expressions. Some still continued dancing.

Kallo had wheeled on Itabi and was pointing at something on the ground. The warriors and women with turtle-shells on their ankles strained to look— *what was it?* On the ground were multicolored hills of corn kernels. All of them looked to have spilled from pouches attached to Itabi's feathered staff.

"We all wanted to trust you," yelled Kallo, *"but we should have known not to trust a spy from the Owl Clan!"*

Itabi looked on wordlessly in horror and disbelief. The realization of what was happening dawned on him. Those pouches of *tanchi* from the old harvest weren't his, and Kallo knew it. Chaos was erupting around them. What had been a united circle only a moment ago had all but fallen apart. *It must be a nightmare, it must be!*

Word of these events quickly reached Shanafila and the Miko. The crowd parted as they made their way to the center of the white-sanded square, nodding at the concerned dignitaries who sat under the arbors.

Tears welled up in the boy's eyes. *"B-b-but...it's not — I didn't...those aren't mine!"*

"What is the meaning of this, Kallo?" demanded Stone Foot through the noise.

"Am I to answer for this outsider's crimes?" Kallo hissed back. *"He has used our Ceremony to make a fool of all of us!"*

"Enough, enough," cried Musholatubih. *"Our sacred dance of the Busk has been interrupted, and for what reason?"*

"Please, I —"

"No! He has shamed the Bear Clan. Can you see, Miko? So little does he think of us that he steals from the crops of our fields — during our fasting — and decorates his staff with his loot. He must be punished!"

A murmur crept through the crowd. Many were restless, only wishing to carry on with the magic of the night's festivities. Others were seeded with suspicion and fear by Kallo's words. Itabi's head was spinning and he leaned on a nearby shoulder for support. His power had deserted him.

"Wait, wait!" A movement rippled through the crowd and a short man with longish hair appeared near the fire. *"It's a misunderstanding, Miko. That staff in Itabi's hands is one I made myself. The pouches of tanchi too, are my own. I neglected to remove them, that's all. Itabi has done no wrong."* It was Ikbi.

Kallo's eyes widened in fury, but Shanafila held up his hand and turned to the Miko. *"Escort the boy* back to his quarters," Musholatubih declared, "and we will discuss this matter with the potter in private. Keep your fires alive. We will continue our Ceremony in the morning!"

Two of the tallest warriors in the Bear Clan took Itabi by the arm and walked him back to Ikbi's hut. Through his angry tears and embarrassment, something had caught his eye and he now strained his neck to catch another glimpse. He recognized that blue hawk on Shanafila's shoulder — it was the same one that had visited him the day before.

Everything else was a furious blur.

•

"Halito! The Sun has risen again to seek its heroes, Itabi. Will it find you today among the living?"

There was only bitter silence in response. Wolf's Friend shifted his weight uncomfortably in the heat. His conscience wouldn't allow him to leave the strange boy on his own — the truth was that Wolf's Friend felt somewhat guilty for not having prevented what had happened.

"Listen, you didn't think that reaching the Emerald Mound would be easy, did you?"

The door of Ikbi's lodge slowly creaked open. Wolf's Friend looked around discreetly before stepping inside. He smiled to himself — the boy certainly hadn't made a secret of his aspirations.

Itabi was sprawled out across his bed of deerskin blankets, staring listlessly at the thatched roof. He was still in his stomp dance regalia from the night before. Dirt and tears had mixed with the paint on his face and the mess was caked around his cheeks. The boy had wept bitterly for much of night; now he was still, hollow as a reed.

"You've allowed your sacred fire to go out," said Wolf's Friend, observing the ashen hearth with disapproval. He turned and exited the lodge. Minutes later, he returned with flaming branches and a heavy jug of water.

"Here, use this to wash your face. You look like death," he added with a chuckle. Itabi did as told, moving like a sleepwalker. Wolf's Friend stoked the struggling flame until the sound of crackling leaves filled the little hut.

"It could've been much worse, you know."

Itabi's eyebrows snapped up incredulously. *"Y-you're joking, right? You must be. My dreams have been shattered. My rep...My reputation ruined. How can you say that?"* He took a draught of water, feeling the cool liquid hit the back of his throat.

"Do you understand," replied Wolf's Friend, *"what could've happened last night, were it not for Ikbi's kindness? You would've received the penalty for stealing corn, right there in front of the whole town. The Sky Elders are clearly watching over you, brother."*

The boy thought about this, then locked eyes with his visitor. *"And Ikbi, w-what has become of him?"*

"He is with the Miko — all is well. The council has decided to withhold punishment. Ikbi is looked upon very highly by Shanafila and the Bear Clan."

Itabi returned his gaze to the ground, taking a deep sigh. *"So is Kallo! How c-can someone who doesn't know me...how can he hate me so much? S-something special was happening around that fire. He...he..."* The boy sobbed, choking back fresh tears.

Wolf's Friend placed his hand on Itabi's shoulder. *"Listen to me, Itabi. You have a special gift — hearing you* sing in the town square showed me that you were named correctly. But there's one thing you need to understand about this gift — it will make others jealous."

"Jealous? But K-Kallo's fame spreads throughout the Seven Clans — "

"And beyond, yes. But when someone has too much of something, he becomes fearful that he will lose it. When Kallo hears the beauty of your voice, he doesn't feel joy. No! He feels threatened — threatened that what you have will make him unimportant."

Itabi could only shake his head in disbelief. Such a perspective seemed alien to him. *How could someone choose to destroy another's Dream in order to pursue his own?*

"You are young, Itabi. If this is a new lesson for you, learn it well. Some people will become poisoned with jealousy when they meet you. They may say or do things that are meant to hurt you. You must not, under any circumstances, become attached to their words or actions — "

"Why not?"

"More often than not, those words or actions have little to do with you. They come from that person's own fears and misunderstandings. They have chosen to build their life from those fears, and that is their own business. Your life, however, is yours to build."

The boy could sense the truth in Wolf's Friend's words. Looking at him there in the dim light of the lodge, Itabi knew the young man spoke with sincerity. He still smarted from the emotional pain of the stomp dance, but Wolf's Friend's words helped him remember who he was. For most of the night, his sorrow had caused him to forget that.

"W-why are you being so kind to me?" he asked.

"Well, you saved my friend from certain death at the hands of the wrong snakeroot," Wolf's Friend said with a grin. "I understand how you must feel, being in a new town and not knowing who to trust. I work under Shanafila; I know Kallo too well. I see all the politics, and it is politics that will be the ruin of the People of One Fire.

I watched your face when Kallo falsely accused you of theft. You were like a baby deer bitten by a rattlesnake. I want you to know that the Emerald Mound is a real place and that there is more than one way of getting there. The *moment we give in to fear is the moment our path becomes lost in the fog. The medicine man told me that, once – "*

As if suddenly remembering something, Wolf's Friend jumped up and announced his departure. Itabi watched him go. There were many decisions to make. *Finding one's self isn't easy*, Bearcloud had said to him weeks ago. Sitting down, Itabi noticed that Wolf's Friend's fire was still burning true.

What a strange thing to say about the Emerald Mound, the boy thought to himself.

•

The harvest moon rose and waned over the great river and its pearls of interconnected towns. Medicine men and high priests guided the people through the old rituals of the Green Corn Ceremony as best they could. *"It's as though,"* they muttered to one another, *"we try to teach children a language that we hardly know ourselves anymore."*

Corn harvests were below average in yield, and trade between the different *talwas* slowed as the usual surplus in crops disappeared. Gone, too, were many of the works of craftsmanship which in the past had always kept the old stories alive. Even the quartz crystals of the oracles, traditionally used to trace the future, only offered blurred images from their silver centers.

Many people spoke in whispers of leaving the river and taking to the road, as in the old times. They were weary of reading the signs that made their home seem like a place of ruin. *"That which once held us together can no longer be found,"* *moaned* one town-crier to his fellow inhabitants. The Seven Clans found themselves on the edge of an abyss.

Chatelan was still conflicted over the events of its Ceremony. For a brief moment, the boy from the Owl Clan had caused the town to levitate. So powerful was his gift that many people ascribed supernatural powers to it. For some, his song at the stomp dance had allowed them to remember tales of legends that had long since faded away with the fires.

Others, sensitive to the world of Spirit, reported hearing the sound of their ancestors walking among the burial grounds at night. They talked about how Itabi's voice had opened a door to a reality unknown to humans, even hidden from them. There were stories of strange lights appearing in the night sky, things that some saw and others didn't.

The scandal at the stomp dance was the cause of much debate. There were those who sided with Kallo, claiming that Itabi was an agent sent to bewitch the people of the Bear Clan. The rumors of an attack on Chatelan by the Owl Clan, now flying red flags of war on its canoes, seemed to support their suspicion.

Kallo's treachery, on the other hand, was no secret. During the third day of the Ceremony, the Sun-Dancer had dislocated the shoulder of a warrior from the Deer Clan during a stickball match. He made no apologies. It was evidence to many in Chatelan of Kallo's reckless ambition and, by extension, his framing of Itabi at the stomp dance.

As a result, a certain aura hung around Itabi. To some he was dangerous, to others he was a savior, and still to others he was a little of both—and an enigma besides. His split with the Sun-Dancers had made him something of a hermit; Itabi was only spotted outside of Ikbi's hut from time to time, helping the craftsman polish and arrange his earthenware.

Some wondered ruefully if he would ever sing again, but felt unsure of how to approach the strange and talented boy. As the fire continued to wither like an autumn leaf, Itabi was both a symbol of hope and confusion for Chatelan. If the elders had any insight, they were keeping it to themselves.

It had been hard for Itabi to deliver the news of his decision to Light Cry. He had never experienced the kind of brotherhood that he felt with the Sun-Dancers. They were his friends, and he wouldn't have been in Chatelan without them. Light Cry tried talking Itabi into changing his decision but in the end, he left his uncle's hut with a downcast expression.

Kallo's untrustworthiness was a big reason why Itabi chose to part with the Sun-Dancers, but there was something else too. As the boy polished Ikbi's ornate pots with a rag, day in and day out, he had time to reflect on what had happened at the stomp dance. He sensed a change in the winds.

Perhaps, he thought, the Great Spirit wants me to move in a different direction. He thought back to when he met the Sun-Dancers in the forest. At first, they were wild deer but in the next moment, they were humans telling jokes and guiding his Dream. Itabi had assumed that their vision of reinvigorating the people during the Green Corn Ceremony was what was right for him. That had changed, too.

It reminded him of something his mother had said to him once. *"The world is always changing, Itabi, but its truths remain the same."* Walking the path of his True Self had led Itabi through many twists and turns and had brought him to crossroads where he felt completely lost. He had even debated leaving Chatelan.

Still, there was always something—a friend, a firefly blinking in the darkness—that reassured Itabi and helped him trust his path. The Sun-Dancers and their breathless visions weren't the only way he could reach the Emerald Mound. Itabi decided to be patient. He committed himself to helping Ikbi manage the business of his pottery.

It turned out that Ikbi was a good friend to have, and not just for his natural kindness. The elders' council of Chatelan frequently commissioned him to craft tobacco pipes and power objects that usually took the form of animals. His work was valued highly by other towns up and down the river and although trade had almost ground to a halt, Ikbi still found himself busy.

Unmarried and known for being a loner, the potter had never had an apprentice like Itabi. In the boy from Chucalissa, he had found a quick learner and able body. Itabi was astounded to see that a clay animal could come from his own hands, it felt like a kind of magic. The first animal Ikbi had instructed him to mold, naturally, was a wolf.

In the beginning, Itabi had tried to shape the wolf's jaw perfectly, but to no avail. He had an idea of how he wanted the wolf to look, but it seemed as though his hands wouldn't obey him. Itabi finally understood how Running Hair felt in her pursuit of painting the perfect sunset.

Ikbi watched in silence. He placed a gentle hand on the boy's shoulder. *"Let the heart work through the hands and your clay will come to life."* Heeding the potter, Itabi soon noticed that a clay wolf had formed between his palms, its nose pointed towards the sky.

"People always want to think their way through living," Ikbi said, *"but anything worth having must come through the heart."* When Itabi went to put the well-sunned clay wolf with Ikbi's other figurines, the artist shook his head. *"Keep it. Your True Self sometimes needs a mirror."*

Slowly, Itabi recovered his resolve under the potter's patient tutelage. He learned to mold tobacco pipes of all shapes and sizes and sometimes took them to the council lodge. Walking around the town, Itabi could even identify which pipes weren't from Chatelan. This knowledge gave him a sense of importance.

His Dream, however, would only let him rest for so long.

•

Part 3

"How is it," Itabi asked one day, "that... that you remember how to make these things when others have forgotten?"

"It's through no skill of my own," said Ikbi in his usual slow manner. When he saw Itabi's curious, unblinking eyes, he pressed on. "There is someone, Itabi, who has been waiting to meet you when the time is right."

"Th-there is?"

"*Hoke*, there is."

Itabi, impatient with Ikbi's terseness, tried to get more out of him. "The time *must* be right, where is this...this someone? Is-Is it a girl?"

Ikbi smiled at Itabi with mischief. "If you fancy me a matchmaker, *holhkopunna*, then your dreams have grown too big."

The potter broke off in a great fit of laughter, tickled with himself. Itabi sighed, unimpressed. Sometimes he *could* see the resemblance between Light Cry and Uncle Ikbi.

"I will see to it," said the potter, regaining himself and concluding the matter, "that he pays us a visit tomorrow."

Itabi sighed again. "Do you think—is it your destiny to be in Chatelan?"

Ikbi, sharpening the end of a wooden stake with a flint knife, looked up at the boy for a moment and then back down to his work again. Itabi saw how the words had changed his mood.

"My duty is here with my people; that is the most I can say."

"Did you always know you would stay in Chatelan, Uncle Ikbi?"

"Not always," the potter replied solemnly. "As a young man, I wanted to travel to the place where the great river drains into the mighty sea. Yes, that is what I wanted! My father would show me the seashells from the tribes of the south — fresh as snow. ,

Sometimes he would let me hold the conch-shells. When I held them to my ear, I heard the roar of the mighty sea. I felt like it was inviting me to come visit its shores. I was filled with excitement." For a moment, Ikbi's face was aglow with the life of his memory with a far-off look in his eyes. "That was the place I wanted to go."

"And w-what happened?"

"I had obligations here in Chatelan with the Miko," Ikbi replied, snapping out of his momentary trance. "Now everything is as it should be, Itabi."

"But...But what about your dream," the boy insisted, "what about the s-seashells and the mighty sea?"

"*Kia*, these were only the fleeting dreams of a young boy before his life began. If I had lived the life of a wanderer, I never would've made all of the beautiful things people know me for. That is my service to the Seven Clans — it is what I was meant to do."

"Are you happy?"

Ikbi went on scraping his knife to the point of the stake with great concentration, not giving Itabi an immediate answer. The boy began to think that Ikbi hadn't heard him and almost repeated the question. "I am satisfied," the potter finally remarked, "for I have shown honor in my decisions."

Later that night, Itabi reflected on what Ikbi had said. Is feeling satisfied the same thing as being happy, the boy thought to himself, or is it another way of saying that one is comfortable in their unhappiness? Itabi once again recalled Bearcloud's words.

The story of 'why not' is driven by people's fear—fear of unacceptance, fear of failure, fear of success. We reject our destiny when we give power to our fears.

The boy wondered how many times Ikbi had told others his story, or even to himself. One thing that Itabi had learned on his journey was the power that stories had over people. A story could control how a person perceives the world around them. Kallo and his tale of the two clans flashed across his mind.

But what if, the boy thought to himself, Uncle Ikbi *had* followed his Dream of visiting the mighty sea? Would it mean that he would've never made those exquisite tribal staffs? Perhaps, Itabi decided, Uncle Ikbi would've created something entirely different, something equally wonderful and profound. It was impossible to know.

Itabi realized for the first time, that had he never left the strawberry meadow, the sycamore tree, his mother's little hut in Chucalissa, he would have never found his voice. The boy thought to himself, my tongue would still be in the way! The emerald necklace, he realized, was the reminder of the agreement he had made with his True Self.

While there were days still, of course, when Itabi still wished his speech was like everyone else's, it didn't upset or embarrass him the way it had before. The power of having a gift to share with the world made his shortcoming seem less significant. He went to sleep that night humming his song from the stomp dance, for the words still lived on his lips.

•

"Itabi, our visitor has arrived."

It was midday and the boy had only just finished a small meal of corn cakes and squash. Itabi hastened to make himself presentable. He had been awaiting this moment with anticipation — which was why it surprised him to see who was stepping into Ikbi's lodge.

"Wolf's Friend!?"

"*Halito*, Itabi. I have someone here who would like to meet you."

Another man stepped in behind Wolf's Friend. His appearance struck Itabi as incredibly peculiar. He was an older man, perhaps older than Ikbi, and he wore a long, dark blue mantle, tall moccasin boots and a starry quartz crystal as a necklace. His eyes shone clearly as his gaze met Itabi's for the first time.

"This is Anoli," said Wolf's Friend by way of introduction.

When Itabi went to greet the stranger, he found himself being interrupted. "Anoli is deaf, Itabi. I am here as an interpreter so the two of you can speak. You are lucky," he added, "that he has come to see you."

Itabi turned again to Anoli and gave a pronounced nod, unsure of what to do. Wolf's Friend put a hand on his shoulder. "To say hello, you go like this," he said, demonstrating by arcing his hand in a waving gesture. Itabi did so, eliciting a deep smile and an answering wave from Anoli. Between his wrinkles, Itabi noticed a long scar along the elder's left temple.

Anoli hadn't been seen in Chatelan for some time, but his life was an object of fascination for many in the Bear Clan. Legend had it that Anoli the Elder came under the influence of *Kwanoka'sha*, a little forest spirit, and had decided to give his voice in exchange for the power to speak with plants and animals. Some even thought that he lived with his own family of changelings.

The visitors sat down with Itabi as the potter prepared cups of water and passed around bowls of mulberries. Itabi found himself fascinated with how clearly Anoli's personality shone through despite the inability to speak. He seemed like an excitable man. Ikbi had directed Anoli's attention to some of his new projects—his earnest reactions now seemed to fill the hut.

"Yesterday," Ikbi addressed Itabi, "you asked how it is that I am able to keep my earthenware faithful to the old designs. If it weren't for Anoli the Elder, none of these things here would exist. He alone granted me the memory of our people when all else seemed lost."

Itabi was mesmerized with the movement of Wolf's Friend's hands as he translated for Anoli. It struck him that people could speak a language without making a sound. Itabi watched Anoli leaning forward as his interpreter signed. The elder started tracing shapes with his forefinger in the dirt of the lodge's floor — the boy craned his neck to get a closer look.

"I, too," continued Ikbi, "felt the terror of our people's traditions slipping from my grasp; my hands moving blindly across the clay. I thought for certain that I would need to find a new skill. And then, like a blessing from the Great Spirit, Anoli began to draw the objects I could no longer find..."

They all looked at the ground where Anoli used his index finger like a paintbrush. His drawing looked to be a tobacco pipe stylized in the form of a woman sitting cross-legged, her head tilted upward, toward the sky. The wash-basin in her lap served as the tobacco bowl, and her thick ponytail the place where smoke was pulled through.

On the other side of the fire, Ikbi held up the embodied tobacco pipe, its shape identical to the one depicted in the dirt. Anoli made a sweeping gesture with a twinkle in his eye. "He says," Two White Feathers explained, "that it should be a little bigger."

Itabi looked from face to face through the laughter. *Why does this man want to speak with me?* Reading the boy's question, Anoli began signing rapidly in Itabi's direction. The boy quieted his thoughts, trying to sense what the man was saying to him—it seemed that Anoli could pick up on what was being said without Wolf's Friend's help.

"They have told me about you," Wolf's Friend interpreted, "and what I have heard about Itabi from the Owl Clan has pleased me, though I am not surprised by his story. You see, there was someone who once told me, a long time ago, 'When you walk with purpose, the Earth is a partner in your Dream.' Those are the words of Shikoba, your grandfather."

"W-wait, you know my—" Itabi, catching himself, pointed at his chest to show his meaning, though the surprise on his face needed no interpretation. Anoli nodded up and down with a grin on his face. Finally understanding, the boy settled in to listen.

•

"I am a man of the forest," Anoli the Elder signed, "and I have learned many of its secrets. I can tell the mood of a mother bear by her tracks in the dirt; I can predict the weather by watching a flock of geese in flight. There is nothing special to it. I am only different because I have spent all my life listening. Every living thing has its own way of speaking, Itabi.

You listen to the world with your ears, but that is only one way of hearing. When I walk into the forest, I can shift my attention from the beetle beneath the ferns to a family of deer that are resting a full day's trek from where I stand. All living things have an inner language and you must be silent to hear it. Man talks and stays on the surface of life, but he is deaf to the world around him.

I've known both your grandfather and Shanafila for a very long time — they were close friends long before they were medicine men. Shanafila saw me speaking with a hawk in the forest, and so he asked me to teach him. Hawks are very suspicious of humans at first, but if you win their trust, they will remain loyal to you. Shanafila learned his lessons well.

Shikoba was different from Shanafila. He was more patient and forbearing. Shanafila always wanted to act on instinct. They both learned from the same medicine men. Shanafila would come to your *talwa*, Chucalissa, and Shikoba would come here to Chatelan. Our clans shared knowledge more freely in those days.

As they matured, both became accomplished medicine men. They had children and took on the responsibilities of fatherhood. Around that time, there was an outbreak of dreams in the Seven Clans. By this I mean about half of the *talwas*, including yours, had a dream of the sacred fire being eclipsed. The other half, including Chatelan, had a dream of the sacred fire being reborn.

Shanafila and Shikoba both read the signs, and they realized that soon the People of One Fire would be facing a catastrophe. They sought me out for advice together. At that time, there was a chant that had been passed down through our medicine men for centuries. It was said to have been bestowed to us from our brothers in the sky, long, long ago.

'If there was some way to record that chant,' they said, 'then our children's children will have the power to replenish the sacred fire, even if their heads have been emptied of memories.' Shikoba had heard tales of strange people in far-off lands who use *talking leaves* to spread their ideas. He thought that creating pictures for our language, as they had for theirs, would help us record the chant.

Shanafila thought the idea a good one, but said that it would take too long. 'Our people have never used such pictures,' he said, 'and we don't know if what works for *hatak inla* would work for us.' He and Shikoba argued this point for some time. When Shikoba returned to Chucalissa, Shanafila's blue hawk followed him, and overheard the comments Shikoba made to the elders.

This was very unfortunate, Itabi, for it created tension between your grandfather and Shanafila. Eventually, they stopped talking to each other altogether. The question of how to record the chant was still unanswered. Shikoba attempted to create pictures for our talking sounds, but it was already too late. With a single thunderclap, our medicine men were silenced, and our chant swept away.

In the case of Shikoba and Shanafila, they were lucky to know me—they already knew how to sign before they lost their speech. This was a blessing from the Great Spirit, for in everything there is balance. Now Shikoba's grandson sits before me, a young man whose voice can do more than any *talking leaves*.

No, I never learned the ancient chant, Itabi, but I know one thing: it was born on the Emerald Mound, and there it will be reborn as well."

•

For days after their first meeting, Itabi saw Anoli's hands moving in a blur as the voice of Wolf's Friend reached his ears. *When you walk with purpose, the Earth is a partner in your Dream.* His grandfather had found a way to speak to him, after all. It filled the boy with warmth to know that both he and his grandfather had followed the same Dream.

Itabi understood his journey in ways he hadn't before, but it only left him with more questions. How could he find a chant lost to the sands of time? If the medicine men had put aside their differences to create a way for the chant to be known, it would be another matter. But they had left nothing, and there wasn't a living person to teach Itabi how to sing it.

That was the other thing, the boy thought to himself. How could he know that he could trust Shanafila? He had started to feel the Chatelan medicine man's eyes on him everywhere he went. The blue hawk seemed to follow Itabi, just as it had followed Shikoba in the past.

Does Shanafila hold a grudge against me for being Shikoba's grandson? What if Kallo acted under his orders to humiliate me?

He already knew that the Sun-Dancers would no longer serve as his path to the Emerald Mound. He also knew that it would be unwise to try and go there alone. There had to be someone, the boy thought, who was both willing to go *and* stay true to their word. Humans were capable of miracles, yes — if only they could get out of their own way.

Anoli the Elder was a constant fascination to Itabi. He said mysterious things which the boy never imagined he'd hear someone say. In explaining his scar, Anoli told Itabi that it was the punishment of a mother wildcat for playing too roughly with her cub. After that, he and the wildcat got over their differences. He really did seem to live in a different world, the boy thought.

Despite his handicap, Anoli could sense far more than other people were able to. How could that be, Itabi wondered to himself. It was almost as though the picture was flipped around—those who *only* used their ears to listen to the living world were at a disadvantage. They were deaf to an entire realm of communication. Maybe that was where the ancient chant could be found.

As Anoli continued to pay visits to Ikbi's lodge, usually in the early afternoon, Itabi began to pick up some of his sign language. He found that learning to express himself with his hands excited him almost as much as singing did. Here is a language, the boy thought, that allows me to talk fluidly, without all the stopping and starting. He felt himself blooming with confidence.

One day, Itabi was sitting with Anoli the Elder as he smoked tobacco from one of Ikbi's pipes. The boy was eager to test his understanding of Anoli's language. He asked a question that had been flickering in his mind for several weeks. Anoli's eyes rested kindly on the boy as he did his best to sign through the question.

"What is the ancient chant, and how is it that the sacred fire can be revived by using it?"

"A long time ago," Anoli started, "when our people had only just arisen from our home inside of the earth, we were visited by our brothers in the sky. They were older than us and had far more wisdom than we did. They wanted to help us. Our people were happy to learn from them. They asked us one question: 'What do you wish to do?' Our answer was, 'we wish to grow.'

They said, 'if that is what you want, we will teach you something that has helped others do the same.' They taught us how the Great Spirit created all the worlds, above and below, with vibration. When they asked if we wanted to know more, we said yes. The brothers in the sky then taught us how we could use sound to create new vibrations.

They asked us if we wanted to know more, and we said yes. The brothers in the sky then taught us how there were patterns of sound that created vibrations of peace, harmony and justice. They told us that creating these sounds would connect us to the True Self and provide for what we need. They asked if we wanted to know more, and we said that was enough."

Itabi, watching Anoli's hands as they flew from one meaning to the next, nodded his head in comprehension. He understood *most* of what Anoli had said. Ikbi smiled and helped fill in some of the missing links. He was impressed with the boy's capacities.

"Anoli," signed Itabi, "when I find this chant, and finally sing it, you won't be able to hear it like the rest of us. Right?"

"I won't need to." The elder smiled. "I can feel everything that ripples from your heart, and for me, that is enough."

•

The river was on fire with the setting Sun's reflection, but Running Hair was running in the opposite direction. There would be no new painting today; she had to find the boy from the Owl Clan. It had been some time since the day they met in the town square. Now the seasons were changing, the air was getting cool, and soon it would be the New Moon Festival.

Running Hair had wanted to speak with Itabi much sooner. As with everyone else in Chatelan, she was riveted by his talent. The girl had thought of his sparkling voice as a midnight sun rising over the stomp dance. She hadn't understood what happened that evening — she only knew that sympathy for the boy moved her heart with the strength of river tides.

The girl was running down the incline of the bluff, darting around the bending paths like a wild mare. "Running Hair, hey!" Her mother's call barely turned her head. Itabi's voice, however, wasn't the reason Running Hair had been hoping to meet him again. Before this moment, she simply wanted to thank him for his idea.

Itabi was right about the value that people attached to her paintings. The eyes of the merchants had lit up when they saw Running Hair's work for the first time. They didn't believe, at first, that the paintings were her own — she was too young for such skill. When Running Hair proved them wrong, she began receiving dyes from local tailors, that she'd only dreamed of.

In the beginning, using the new colors was such a shock that Running Hair felt like she'd stolen the Great Spirit's paints. Her buckskins began to glow with the perspectives from Sunset Bluff in a way she'd never seen. Now there were violets, different blues, and joyful yellows. It became fashionable for people in Chatelan, Chucalissa, and even the *talwas* of the Raccoon Clan to hang up her paintings.

Running Hair bounded through the palisade gates of Chatelan, brushing past the town-crier who sat dozing on a rock. "*Hale!* Have you gone crazy, little girl?" She didn't pay him any mind. With passing interest, the town-crier noticed something jolting up and down on her back. The sleepy corridor of huts absorbed her without a sound and he shrugged his shoulders.

There were people who said Running Hair's paintings possessed their own power. Some reported that, when they woke up in the night to relieve themselves, the pictures seemed to glow with their own mysterious light. Demand for Running Hair's paintings increased, and because she still could not find satisfaction, she continued happily trading them for materials.

The girl found herself in a maze of unfamiliar huts. If Itabi hadn't been sitting outside, working with his pottery, she may never have found him in time. The galloping footsteps startled Itabi out of his careful work. Looking up, he saw the girl who painted sunsets, her face pink and her hair askew.

"Ita...I...I..." Running Hair, gasping for breath, struggled to get her sentence out.

"Now you know how I feel," Itabi grinned.

She took the long cedar flute, slung to her back like a sheaf of arrows, and placed it in the boy's hands. "He...He wanted...He wanted you to have this," she said, panting.

Itabi looked at Running Hair quizzically. "Who did?"

"Bearcloud," replied the girl.

"Bearcloud?!"

"I met him...at...Sunset Bluff."

"Where is he? W-What did he say?"

"He's already gone...He said...He said he had many things to do."

"I'll go find him!"

"He told me you would say that," the girl said, rolling her eyes.

"I-I mean it! I need his help with something, it's urgent—"

"But Bearcloud didn't come to see you this time," said Running Hair, "he came to see me."

Itabi looked at the girl in disbelief, unsure of what to say. His hands closed around the cedar flute in his hands. He noticed white feathers hanging from it.

"Itabi, he had a message for you."

"What is it?"

"You need to leave Chatelan. You need to leave as soon as you can!"

"Why?" The boy's chest was pounding.

"It's the Owl Clan, Itabi. They're preparing to attack us in Chatelan. Everyone will think that you were part of their plan and...and...you just need to leave!"

"The Owl Clan?" He looked at Running Hair in alarm. "That's impossible!"

"*Hale!* The impossible is happening. What will you do?"

The boy buried his face in his hands. "C-Can they really be this stupid?" He imagined the faces of the Owl Clan warriors, twisted with hate, storming the palisades of Chatelan with sharpened arrows poised to kill.

"He said," ventured Running Hair timidly, "that your people are desperate. Soon the frosts will close in, and without the sacred fire it will be a long, long winter. They think the Bear Clan—they think we've cursed them." The girl suppressed a sob in her chest. "They don't understand!"

"Neither do I," said Itabi bitterly. In fact, he *did* understand, and that's what scared him the most. He remembered all too well the warriors' words at the council lodge in Chucalissa. They raised the kind of fear that brought spears out of their hiding places. This time, it seemed, his mother's voice wasn't enough to put them back.

"Wait," said Itabi, seeing that Running Hair was turning to leave. "What did Bearcloud say to you?"

"He said that if I wasn't fed up and frustrated with my paintings, then I wouldn't be on the right path. 'How comforting', I thought to myself. And he gave me this paintbrush—I don't know, it seemed silly."

"I'll bet it's a special paintbrush."

"He also said that when a living thing, person or animal, shows up on your path, to see them for the guides they are."

"Ah, that's nice." Itabi felt his ears go hot.

"My paintings are everywhere because of you — *yakoke*. Please don't get hurt."

"*Hoke*."

With that, Running Hair raced into the dusk. The boy wished that someone like *her* could have power — someone who didn't care about power at all.

•

By the time Itabi had gathered himself to leave Chatelan, it was too late. The warriors from Chatelan closed in around him as he reached the town's east entrance. Midnight shadows hid their faces but the boy could see they were painted red — the color of war. Itabi felt himself seized with panic. When he tried to run, he was tripped and his chin hit the dirt.

"*Halito*, Itabi," sneered the voice of Kallo behind him. "You wouldn't be on your way to visit your friends from Chucalissa, would you?"

Two warriors roughly pulled the boy up from the ground, pinning his arms behind his back. For a moment, he found himself face to face with the Sun-Dancer. His chin still ached from the impact of the fall.

"You don't know what you're doing, Kallo," Itabi said, looking his adversary straight in the eye.

"The game is over," Kallo hissed in response, "your little story of the Emerald Mound is charming but it will get you no further with my people. You knew the plan all along, didn't you? And you still had the nerve to pose as a *na lakancha!*" He spat at Itabi's feet in disgust.

"You're wrong," Itabi, trembling, shot back, "I've remained true to my word, but you were never true to yours."

"You want to talk of being true," roared Kallo, "when we find you sneaking through the gates like a scheming fox? That is the character of your clan, is it not?" He wheeled around and began walking away. "Tie the traitor up in the council lodge!" he yelled without looking back.

Itabi tried to squirm his way out of the hands of the warriors, but their grip was like stone. He felt something cold and sharp press into his neck. "Easy there, owl-boy," one of his captors snickered behind his ear. The boy's shoulders went slack and he hung his head in defeat.

He marched lifelessly into the council lodge. Its damp, earthen odor filled his nose. The warriors ordered him to sit; he felt his wrists being tied together by rope behind his back. They filled his ears with warnings but Itabi barely heard them. Soon, he was alone again in the darkness.

From the leader of the stomp dance, the boy thought to himself, to a prisoner of war. His mind gradually went blank again. Everything had happened so fast that he felt like his thoughts were moving through an algae-thick swamp. Itabi realized that he was waiting for something else to happen. *Maybe Ikbi, or Light Cry would...?* But no one came.

For the second time that night, Itabi felt himself seized with panic. He let desperation take over his movements. He thrashed at the ropes like a cornered animal, straining his body forward to free his wrists.

The knots wouldn't give. Having gained nothing, Itabi finally gave in to exhaustion. He slept without being sure that he was sleeping.

The first prelude of dawn came — it found the boy with his head slumped into his chest. He awoke with a start, listening. Drums of war were vibrating through Chatelan. Itabi looked at the ashen hearth at his feet. The night had been cold and his limbs were stiff; there was no fire. The Bear Clan warriors must have already set out, the boy thought with a shiver.

His thoughts turned to his native town and his mother's safety. *What am I doing in the enemy's territory?* Itabi shook off the question as soon as it crossed his mind. It wasn't the enemy that was the problem, but the idea that there was an enemy at all. He was imprisoned by a story whose vocabulary was fear and pride. People suffered, he realized, from words born out of fear.

Itabi could feel it everywhere, feeding off itself and getting bigger. An elder came to take him outside; everything seemed to be red. People's faces, the banners flying atop the palisades, the flint blades and copper axes — all red. Itabi understood, then, that war was a symptom of fear. The people's custom of red paint was only a symbol of that fact.

The elder, grim and iron-muscled, kept a close watch as the boy answered the call of nature. If the prisoner were to take off and escape, he would have to answer for the mistake. Itabi, however, showed no signs of trickery. He was allowing himself the chance to listen to what he felt around him, as Anoli had counselled only days ago.

The silence of the town square was eerie. There was a stillness that made the boy's heart skip a beat. Only the women and children were left behind and they clung to one another in their huts. War had robbed Chatelan of its life-force. He and the elder were trudging back, finally, when Itabi froze.

He found himself looking at two girls huddled around their little brother in a doorway. Their faces, too, were painted red—almost like the masks worn by the dead when they were buried. There was no joy in those faces, even though a child's face was where joy was supposed to live. Only fear, the boy thought to himself.

Itabi thought of all the generations before him that grew up like that; who, for one reason or another, were forced to wear a mask of dread and unhappiness. A great sadness swept over him that was far greater than any self-pity he'd felt. Humans created a world that was always hurting because their hearts cried for healing. That was the way it was—or, at least, the way it had been.

Back in the council lodge, the ropes digging into his skin, the boy thought only of how he could bring happiness to the children's faces. For most of his journey, Itabi had been concerned with proving himself. He had wanted to show everyone that he was good enough. Now that idea seemed as distant as last summer's worn-out clothing.

Anoli had talked about the brothers in the sky and their vibrations of peace. The boy wasn't sure what was true and what was story. It wouldn't surprise him if there *were* people in the stars who also came from the Great Spirit. After all, who could know? He knew for certain, though, that what the story meant was true.

At that very moment, warriors of the Owl Clan and Bear Clan were clashing somewhere down the river. Bows were drawn, spears were flashed, conch-shells rattled, and lives lost. Itabi wondered where Shanafila and his blue hawk were, whether they knew where *he* was. He wondered if the old high priest thought that his pride was worth the blood being spilled.

Itabi's emerald necklace, meanwhile, was starting to behave strangely. He hadn't noticed it at first with the rest of his body being so uncomfortable, leaned over in front of the lodge's central pillar. He had slipped in and out of consciousness as the day wore on. But he noticed that there was a warmth around his throat. When he looked down, he saw the stone was lit up like a green star.

The earthen walls seemed to collapse in on themselves and spin in circles. Itabi lost track of time and found himself in a delirium. At times he thought that he heard Bearcloud's flute; and at other times, Opa's voice as she pounded roots into powder. *Has it been a day, or only an hour?* The warmth of the emerald necklace, vibrating at his throat, was the only thing he could feel.

When an arrow sang by his left ear and then by his right, Itabi thought he was only dreaming. He realized his ropes were severed and he bolted to his feet. All he could see in front of him was a tall shadow, standing motionless.

•

"You don't understand," protested Wolf's Friend, "this chant of our ancestors is like a wild stag that must be caught from the air. Who else will catch it besides Itabi?"

"That may be so," replied Two White Feathers, "but there is nothing we can do but follow Shanafila's orders for now. What are you suggesting, that we kidnap the boy from our own war chief and sneak him to the Emerald Mound?"

The two young men sat in their bear furs next to a gushing spring in the depths of the forest. The cool season of *onafapi* had crept into the river valley and given the woodlands a brief carpet of red and gold. A single leaf twirled in the air and landed in the water, riding the currents out of sight.

"You see," remarked Wolf's Friend, "what were the chances that, out of all the leaves on all the trees in this forest, we'd see that particular one fall? It is the same with our chances of receiving the chant without Itabi."

"But we *did* see it, nonetheless."

"You fail to see my meaning," Wolf's Friend scoffed. The interpreter splashed his face with water, then directed his gaze to the treetops. "Sometimes I wonder how it really is with Shanafila..."

Two White Feathers paused, then looked at his companion. "Care to explain?"

"I think there are two parts of him in conflict. He tried to protect his rival's grandson from his own during those summer months. He saw that Itabi's heart was pure. He made sure Ikbi came to Itabi's rescue at the Ceremony. But he didn't stop Kallo, either—"

"Yes, because he couldn't oppose Kallo with force. He could only reduce the damage of Kallo's actions and wait—"

"For an opportunity to teach his grandson a lesson, *hoke*...an opportunity that never came. Shanafila has good intentions, but don't you think he may feel some satisfaction in seeing Itabi caught in misfortune?"

"There may be a kernel of truth to what you're saying," Two White Feathers responded, "but I think you overreach, *ankana*. We are under attack and the sacred fire is all but quenched. Our clan's medicine man wouldn't play that kind of game with so much at stake."

Wolf's Friend's eyes narrowed in silence.

"He said," Two White Feathers continued, "that the Great Spirit would take care of Itabi's passage to the Emerald Mound — we just have to make sure *we* get there. That is the only thing we can control."

"May it be so."

The two young men were quiet, listening to the peaceful sound of the stream. Shanafila would meet them soon to begin the trek. Secretly their thoughts wandered to the wellbeing of their friends walking the war-path, but neither man dared to speak of it.

"How many days of a walk is it to this place?"

"I am not sure. Truthfully, I didn't even know of its existence till recently."

"*Hoke.* Neither did I."

•

"Who's there?"

The shadow stepped forward. Itabi's eyes adjusted and he let out a gasp. He realized that he was looking at a woman whose appearance more resembled a man's. Her hair was cropped short so that the angles of her cheekbones stood out. She wore breechcloth leggings tucked into moccasin boots, a yellow leather tunic, feather earrings and a dagger at her hip.

"I am Fala," she said, lowering her bow.

The boy felt his blood run cold. "Fala...how…?"

"Let's save introductions for later," she said crisply. "Are you the boy who wears the emerald necklace?"

Itabi instinctively clutched at the stone on his throat, still warm.

"Well then, you have no idea what it's taken for me to find you."

Itabi looked at the woman, bewildered. "You know who I am?"

"Only what my dream told me—which, inconveniently, was very little." Fala's eyes darted to either side. "There isn't time for talk now."

She retrieved her two arrows and cut the other ropes from Itabi's wrist in one motion. They huddled next to the doorway of the council lodge, peering outside. It was twilight. The red banners fluttering atop the palisades were the only sign of life. Fala gave Itabi a glance; in the next moment, their feet were flying towards the western gate of the *talwa*.

The boy had hoped their escape might be more tactical. Instead, they were running out in the open, attracting attention from townspeople who sat in the void of where the sacred fire once had been. He felt all of his senses in an uproar of alarm. They were being pursued and, worse still, Fala wasn't running towards a gate—she was headed straight for the solid wall itself.

"Hey! There's no opening here!"

Fala's momentum remained unchanged. Twisting his neck around, Itabi saw that their pursuers had stopped short to load their bows. His legs started to lag in despair. The boy was ready to surrender when he noticed tufts of feathers sprouting from Fala's arms, like plants. One arrow whizzed by them, and then another.

"Climb up to the top," yelled Fala, scaling the palisade wall with unnatural alacrity.

Itabi struggled to hoist himself up along the rough texture of the bark. Fala grasped the boy by the arm and began pulling him up to the edge. Something sharp caused pain to shoot up and down his calf; he almost lost his grip. Itabi wondered if death had chosen to meet him here.

"You're almost there!"

Fala's face was becoming narrower, the copper skin of her arms obscured by white feathers. Itabi's amazement gave him a surge of courage. The two were now standing alongside the banners of the palisades, overlooking the river. The men's arrows stopped; they couldn't understand what they were seeing.

"Itabi, are you ready?" Fala was lowering herself into a crouch, indicating for the boy to straddle her back. *The magic begins when you trust yourself enough to take a chance.* As soon as he put his arms around her plumed neck, Fala jumped into the air with a strength that felt not of this world.

For a moment, they were two humans in the air, vulnerable to the earth's gravity. They were plummeting towards the sandy shore; Itabi shouted without knowing it. And then the boy's entire world changed. Two outstretched arms became beating, cloud-white wings—suddenly, they were lifting upwards into the evening sky, light as dandelion seeds.

Itabi was so astonished, at first, that he felt himself on the verge of fainting. He clung to the giant bird's neck until his knuckles were white. His eyes were squeezed shut; he didn't dare move a muscle. The boy opened his eyes to slits and, beyond the down of the bird's neck, caught sight of a long, winding snake spanning the earth below. It was the great river.

The boy relaxed, and he began to laugh. He laughed like he never had before. Everything he'd wanted to share with his mother came out in his laughter. He held out his hand to watch how it passed through floating puffs of clouds and laughed harder. I am free, the boy thought to himself. His face was wet with tears—the laughter was a kind of crying, too.

As Itabi and Fala soared above it, Chatelan was already murmuring with the tale. Its people would soon count their dead and dig at the ashy mounds in their huts in vain. The story of the woman who changed into a white raven offered a ray of hope, even if some didn't believe it to be true.

It made its rounds between the *talwas* of the Deer Clan, the Raccoon Clan, and even Chucalissa. "These are dark times," they whispered, "but perhaps White Raven Woman is a sign that the Great Spirit hasn't forgotten about the People of One Fire." The tale reached Opa's ears, too; she had waited so long to smile.

Opa knew the story was only a beginning, both for the Seven Clans and her son, still flying the path of his vision quest.

•

"I've never seen someone do that before," the boy ventured shyly.

Fala, back in her human form, said nothing. They were outside of her log house, surrounded by a grove of tall gums and amber sycamores. She was applying an ointment to Itabi's leg where the arrow had grazed him. He was lucky, she told him. He'd lost only a little blood.

"Is it a secret, the way you're able to fly like that?"

"It is for those to know who must know," the young woman replied. She glanced up at Itabi, sensing his disappointment. "Anyone can fly. Most people believe they can only walk, and so that is what they do."

Giving his leg a final tap, Fala picked up a basket of pecans and squatted against the log house to deshell them. Itabi took a gulp of water from her gourd, surprised at his own thirst. He found it hard to believe that anyone could change into a bird when they wanted.

"Could I learn to fly?"

"That is entirely up to you," Fala said, cracking a pecan open.

"Maybe I don't understand."

"For me," Fala sighed, "it was something that happened out of necessity. At least, that's the way it appeared at first. And—" She suddenly paused and gave the boy a sharp look. "Are you sure you want to listen?"

The boy nodded excitedly.

"This is a story I keep to myself, normally. *Hoke.* I had a little brother named Hanan whom we loved very much. He was always sick. I remember always having to run out to get medicine when my grandmother asked me to. She said his spirit kept reaching for heaven.

One day, his face was very pale and his fever was very high. He didn't respond to my grandmother's medicine. She said we needed the bark from an old cedar tree to save him, but that the trees were very far away. There wasn't enough time. I listened to my mother and father wail, and I couldn't bear it.

I ran outside, and I ran and ran. I realized that I needed wings, and I kept running. There were ravens flying above me. I remembered what my grandmother had told me once: *Your destiny is someone who is looking for you. Your words are the bright colors that help it find you in the darkness.*

I was pumping my arms faster and faster, and I shouted, 'I am ready to walk on the air, I am ready to fly!' I was connecting with the ravens and their breath became my own. That is the best way I can tell it to you. The next thing I knew, I was in the air, looking down at the treetops for the first time."

"And your brother?"

We kept Hanan with us that time, and we were very happy. But he didn't stay on earth for much longer. In that moment, we were together as a family. We ate grape dumplings and fry bread and counted our blessings from the Great Spirit." Fala paused as the memory passed through her heart like a spring breeze.

"That is how I became a Dream Guide, anyway, and that is what's important." She held out a rabble of pecans in her hand. "Try some."

Itabi savored the crunchy treat. He was happy to be in the woodlands again, where he had first discovered his gift. The air was crisp; he drew his shawl of deerskin tightly around his shoulders. As best he could, Itabi explained to his companion why her name had given him such a shock. Fala listened quietly.

"I am a Dream Guide," the young woman said, "I am not responsible for these kinds of coincidences, brother. I cannot tell you that your Fala and *this* Fala are one and the same. I can only say this: hold those coincidences close to your heart, they are messages from your True Self. My mission was to find the boy with the emerald necklace. That's all I knew."

A dry rustling in the leaves attracted the pair's gaze; they agreed it was a snake of some kind, maybe a cottonmouth, and they were comfortable to watch its trail wind in the opposite direction.

"Were my colors bright enough?" Itabi asked suddenly. Fala looked at him questioningly, not understanding. "You said our words are the bright colors that help—" He broke off as Fala started chuckling.

"I found you, didn't I? That's all you need to know. Soon, you will be in the place your path has been leading you to...much better than that dusty old lodge, right?"

The boy nodded shyly. It was remarkable, he thought to himself, how he kept meeting the most mysterious people, and how they all seemed genuinely interested in him. Where had they been all his life? It felt like being part of a Spirit Clan that he was only just learning existed.

"And Hanan? Does he ever visit you in your travels?"

"If he didn't," Fala smiled, "I wouldn't be here with you right now."

•

All night, the wind whispered through the cracks of the loghouse. Itabi had been half-asleep when he heard the rustling of wings just outside. Turning over, he saw that Fala's bed was empty. He sprang to his feet and opened the door, just enough to peek through. The white raven's wings were glowing in the moonlight as it rose over the clearing, into the darkness.

The next thing Itabi knew, it was morning and Fala was gently shaking him awake. "*Ma,* it is time we begin," she was saying. The boy sat up and rubbed his eyes. He could see that Fala was moving with purpose, almost impatiently. *Had it all been a dream?* Itabi threw his blankets aside and planted his feet on the ground.

"Drink this," she said, thrusting a clay cup containing a dark liquid into his hands. The boy gulped it down and felt energy coursing through his body. He realized that he had no desire for food. "Don't forget your flute," Fala added. The two stepped outside. It was an overcast morning and the leaves swirled between the old sycamores.

"Today, we walk to Dancing Bear Creek and begin your initiation. Do you remember the story of the Green Corn Goddess?"

Itabi had to admit that he didn't.

"It is important for you to know it now," Fala said. "A long time ago, the people were in a similar situation as they are today. They were facing a long winter of starvation; no one could find food. There was talk that the Great Spirit had left them behind. Finally, two brave hunters grew tired of this and set out to find food. One of them was the chief's son.

After many days, all they had to show for their trouble was a single bird. They were both weak, hungry and nearing despair. The two hunters came to a great mound. Atop the mound they saw a woman, dressed in white. She asked them if they had any food to share. With no hesitation, they handed over their catch.

That was to their own benefit! She thanked them and said their kindness would be repaid. They watched in amazement as the woman in white began to rise off the mound and into the sky. In her place was a tall, green plant, as green as the lowlands. Its strands of silk were her hair, its yellow kernels the pearls around her neck.

This is how the people were given the gift of *tanchi*, and we celebrate her gift every harvest. Itabi, tell me, where is it that you wish to go?"

"The Emerald Mound."

"And what is it that you wish to find there?"

"The Emerald Chant."

"Then you must bring a gift."

The boy hadn't thought of that. "W-What can I bring?"

"Take your flute," instructed Fala, "and bury it next to Dancing Bear Creek. I will give you six sticks of rivercane. Every morning, bury one stick. When the pouch is empty, return to the creek, and you will be prepared for your initiation."

"But," the boy protested, "I can't bury this flute! It was a..."

"A gift?" Fala smiled. "Remember...the path requires that you make clear decisions – sometimes that means parting with something you love."

Itabi was amazed to hear Bearcloud's words coming from her lips. He accepted the wisdom in Fala's instructions, even if he didn't understand them. They reached the creek and the boy placed the cedar flute in the ground. He felt a tinge of regret as he began to cover it with dirt. He'd never gotten to play it.

The boy did as he was told on the first morning, the second and the third. He buried one stick of rivercane after another near Fala's log house. As his pouch became lighter, he noticed that he felt more nervous. *What initiation is White Raven Woman speaking of?* By now, Itabi had learned the virtue of trust. He was still learning to deepen that trust into faith.

The Emerald Chant. He had never said those words together before, and he wasn't sure what had made him do so with Fala. It was the first time his Dream had announced itself in words. He said them aloud, noticing how they shimmered in the air. Where would the chant come from, he wondered. Before the stomp dance, at least, Itabi had known the song he would sing.

On the fourth day, Fala found Itabi chipping away at a piece of bark with a knife, deep in thought. She could see him feeling the weight of his people's suffering and sat down next to him. Neither of them broke the forest silence for a long time.

"Itabi, do you think you've changed during your journey?"

The boy looked up, surprised. "*Hale!* Of course, I have changed."

"How so?"

"In the beginning, I could barely speak. I didn't even know I could sing."

Fala nodded. "Do you think that, back in your old town, you would've believed someone had they told you who you would become?"

"No, I...I couldn't have imagined any of this."

"And so why is it that you give yourself such a hard time now? So what, if you don't know what will happen at that mound-place? Your heart is capable of things your mind can't imagine, that's all that matters. You speak beautifully to my ears, you know."

Itabi looked at his companion in wonder.

"Why don't you let me hear something? You know, in that magical voice of yours..."

The boy touched the emerald stone at his throat. He realized that it had been a long time since he had sung even a note. His Sun-Dancer friends crossed his mind and he let out a laugh. Fala prodded him again, watching how his energy changed. Itabi sang the Grandmother Spider song, remembering their adventure at the Elders' Gate — it seemed so *long* ago.

"Ah," said Fala afterward, struggling for words, "I wish I could do that."

"But you can fly!" Itabi cried.

"Yes," replied Fala, "but you make *others* fly. That is some powerful medicine."

●

The sixth morning came and Itabi's pouch was finally empty. As they walked to the creek, thunder rolled deeply from the heart of the morning. The pumpkin-colored leaves crunched under their moccasins; only the pine trees retained the summer's greens. Itabi wondered how Anoli would experience this moment in the forest, what song he would hear the earth sing.

The boy had seen the white raven in flight again on the previous day. This time it was circling over the grove, nearing the ground with each turn. Something about the ginger motion of its wings suggested it was hurt. Itabi watched as the white raven landed. Its feathers withdrew into human skin and its shape contracted, like a mirage, until Fala stood in its place.

She knelt there for some minutes, trying to catch her breath. Her gait had looked wobbly as she walked past the log house, into the woods. The boy wondered if something had happened during her time in the air. Fala looked normal as they made their way to Dancing Bear Creek—only her face was very pale.

"You're OK, aren't you?"

"Oh, you noticed," answered Fala, attempting a smile.

"Is something wrong?"

"I am a Dream Guide," she said, "but we also feel the loss of the sacred fire. The forces of the land and the stars are imbalanced. But that is only temporary," she added with a nod of her head. They had reached Dancing Bear Creek.

"Itabi, do you see the spot where we buried your flute?"

The boy looked; he breathed in sharply. Next to the creek was a tall stalk of *tanchi*—its long stalks crowned with plumes of silk. It was taller than either of them and stood swaying in the breeze. The plant had grown to full size from the spot where they had buried Bearcloud's flute. Itabi turned to Fala, but she raised a silencing hand.

"Your questions will be answered one day, but I am not the one to answer them, brother. This is what I can tell you—" Fala paused as a crack of thunder sounded in every direction. "Take the largest husk. When you reach the mound, offer it as a gift to the ones who watch over us, and they will be pleased. After that, you will know what to do."

The boy did as he was instructed. He snapped the largest husk from the stalk of the *tanchi* plant, placing it in his knapsack. The weight of the ripe grain was satisfying. His eyes lifted up again to the head of the plant. *When you walk with purpose, the Earth is a partner in your Dream.*

"Itabi," Fala spoke, "it is time to talk about your initiation. Understand, that will be as far as I can take you. You will finish the path on your own."

"*Hoke*. But won't you join me at the Emerald Mound?"

"My path doesn't go there," she replied. "Now listen! Tell me the meaning of your name."

"The howling of wolves," the boy answered. A soft pattering of leaves announced the first raindrops.

"No names are given by accident, Itabi. The time has come to fulfill yours. Tonight, there will be a full moon—it will hang like a giant persimmon in the sky. The wolves will sing its praises. You will be among them."

"I will?"

"Well, are you opposed to singing with our brother wolves?"

"But won't they attack me?"

"Not if your voice becomes indistinguishable from theirs, they won't." Fala paused. "Have you forgotten, Itabi? Every stone, plant, tree, river, and animal vibrates with the power of the Great Spirit. Humans, too. We all live in the Circle of One, together. Our gifts are here to remind one another that 'brother, sister, we are of the same Circle.'"

"Yes, that is true," Itabi reflected, stroking his chin.

"Sing so that they recognize you, Itabi. After all, you are named after them, aren't you?"

The pattering of raindrops became the crashing of a shower. Fala whooped with joy and began dashing back toward the log house. Itabi followed her in a burst of movement, but then suddenly stopped short. He remembered his dream of the first Fala; how she ran ahead of him on a path. The boy realized he was looking at the same image.

•

It starts with one voice. Lonesome, chilling, true. If the sky is sleeping, it wakes up and listens. One voice becomes many voices. It is the same call echoing through many throats, the call of our ancestors. We all know it. We were born knowing it. The Creator gave us his song because, in the beginning, there was no one else to sing.

We promised that we would sing it for him through the ages.

It is good to sing this song for all the creatures to hear. That way, they remember the Creator. It starts with one voice, and one voice becomes many. A-h-h-w-o-o-o-o! A-h-h-w-o-o-o-o! That is how he taught us. He said, if one sings, all must sing. The song is stronger that way. No one is left out. If one howls, another must answer.

The story of the land and the sky is told in our wails.

Man used to listen to that story. Then he talked so much that his ears changed, and he forgot how to listen. We had waited for one of his sons, one of his daughters to come to us. Others had come, but they did not come to listen, they did not come to sing. Then a young one of theirs appeared and we saw him for who he was.

He had a good heart and something that looked like starlight on his throat.

It starts with one voice. One voice becomes many voices. We gathered around him, and waited. At first, he didn't know us. He didn't understand our ways. There was fear in his heart, and fear always steals the place where hope is supposed to sit. Then, he knew. A-h-h-w-o-o-o-o! The Creator's call lived in his throat, too.

We threw our heads back and answered.

Our call sang through every creature's bones. The moon heard its sadness and wept. And so the young one sang out again, and once again we answered. We watched him dance and saw that our medicine was his. We watched him dance and saw him change into the form of our people.

His color was moon-white and he was bigger than the rest of us.

Our ancestors had known him, and they knew he would return to visit us again. The young one hadn't known that his people and ours were one and the same, and he was joyous when he learned that. He led us in a dance that went in a great circle. If one sings, all must sing. A-h-h-w-o-o-o-o!

And then another of the young one's kind joined in, and we saw that he was a Spirit-Walker.

His fur was also white, but he was much older and his coat was yellowed. The young one stopped and stood still as the Spirit-Walker drew up alongside him. Our people could see that they were one and the same, that they had been apart for a long time. The older one nudged the young one with his snout. They butted heads in greeting, then parted.

Our people understood that the dance must continue.

The Spirit-Walker pointed his nose to the moon. A-h-h-w-o-o-o-o! A-h-h-w-o-o-o-o! The young one answered the call, and so did we. One voice becomes many voices. The dance went on, and there came a time when the young one saw that his elder had vanished.

Now he howled in mourning, and so did we.

We heard that the elder's voice still mingled with ours, and so did he. Our last notes ended in triumph and our tired souls were happy.

It starts with one voice, and all voices become one.

•

When Itabi awoke, his companions had vanished, but he was not alone. A circle of humans surrounded him and the Sun glared into his eyes. Someone's hand pulled him to his feet. He tried to make sense of the faces that he saw. They were daubed in white paint. Itabi slowly recognized the faces, but his understanding lagged behind.

"Itabi! It is Colesqua, your Miko. You have arrived, my son."

The boy's eyes widened. Standing at the chief's side were Shanafila and the Miko of the Bear Clan. Behind them he recognized Two White Feathers and Wolf's Friend. There were hunters from both the Bear

Clan and the Owl Clan, and others he didn't recognize. They were all together, somehow, regarding Itabi with a mixture of warmth and wonder.

"Where am I?" Itabi asked, rubbing his eyes. He didn't believe what he saw could be possible.

"Just beyond this clearing," explained Colesqua, gesturing with his staff, "is the Emerald Mound."

Itabi followed the Miko's line of vision and could see how the forest appeared to open up to a sprawling green hill. He felt his heart skip a beat.

"We have been waiting for you, my son."

"But Miko, I am confused. I thought our clans were still at war. How...?" Itabi trailed off as his gaze met Shanafila's.

"They *are* still at war," Colesqua replied grimly, "but it is the war councils of our respective clans that have chosen that path. We have come together as a secret peace council, an envoy to the Emerald Mound. It is our feeling that the Great Spirit wishes for us to resolve things differently."

Before he could answer, Itabi found himself interrupted by a familiar voice. "*Please!* Hey, *Please!*" It was Light Cry, running up from behind the others. The two embraced ardently. In a time of war, such reunions were never guaranteed.

"*Ankana,* you look different. How is it with you? You leave Chatelan on wings and join the wolves for the full moon, is that right? Never a dull moment, indeed!" The Sun-Dancer was rocking back and forth, almost unable to contain his glee.

"My brother, it brings me joy to see you," said Itabi and smiled. "We will talk of everything soon. Allow me a moment..."

He bowed his head in reverence to the Miko and walked to where Shanafila was standing. The medicine man's blue hawk flashed its wings. To everyone's amazement, the boy from Chucalissa addressed Shanafila in sign language.

"You never forgave my grandfather, isn't that true?"

"So you have heard the story. It is true that our friendship was strained when your grandfather passed. I've always wished that things had happened differently."

"In Chatelan, I felt that you worked against me. You know I am his grandson."

"Your medicine is strong, Itabi. We understood who you were early on. The problem was my grandson. He put himself before the people. Such a person, with his reputation, injures unity."

"They speak of Shikoba and Kallo," announced Mishtubolih to the others.

Colesqua smiled at Itabi. "You saw your grandfather last night, didn't you?"

Itabi nodded in awe. He had almost lost sight of the vision, like a dream that becomes a loose feather in the wind.

Shanafila touched him on the shoulder. "We are here now, by the power of the Great Spirit. This fighting sickens me. The real fight happens inside of us, Itabi. We have all won our battles to come here. We all walk the path of the People of One Fire."

Itabi listened to the medicine man's message and was satisfied. It was all behind them now. They moved as a group in the direction of the green hill.

The men traded tales of their journeys and listened to one another in bemusement. They all felt a special brotherhood that went beyond the identities of their clans. Finally, they gained the lip of the forest.

The boy took a deep breath and exhaled. He was looking at the Emerald Mound. No longer was his Dream something that danced in his mind—it was the very shape of the earth, towering in front of him. It had a smell, a feeling, an allure. The Mound was different than he had pictured, imperfect. At its summit, facing north, was a smaller mound and it called out his name. *Ih-tah-bee.*

"You remember that evening of the council meeting, don't you?"

The boy, startled, looked up at the Miko of the Owl Clan. "Yes, I remember."

"You have fulfilled your name," spoke Colesqua, "but, for our people, that will only be part of the story. We have waited lifetimes for the gift that you now choose to share."

The two natives of Chucalissa continued gazing at the Emerald Mound and were silent. They watched as the blue hawk soared over its apex, spiraling higher and higher into the sky.

•

It was dusk; the ceremony was about to begin. The two mikos sat at the summit of the Emerald Mound in prayer. One wore the face of an owl around his neck, the other wore the face of a bear. They donned white mantles of buckskin and crowns of feathers in their hair. The rest of the council stood in a circle around its base, heads bowed in reverence.

Itabi and Light Cry sat together at a small distance, taking in the views of the hilltop. They had spoken for a long time without realizing it. Much had happened, and there weren't enough words, it seemed, to speak of everything.

"You're so different now, I can't believe it," commented Light Cry. He pinched the fuzz on Itabi's chin—Itabi playfully batted his hand away.

"I remember," the Sun-Dancer continued, "at the Elder's Gate, one of us had said to you: 'If you can sing, then sing.' It gives me chills thinking about that now." He caught Itabi's eyes wandering to the praying mikos at the summit.

"There is no one who will interrupt you today, *hohlkopunna,*" he laughed, getting up. The two embraced, and Itabi began the long walk across the hilltop towards the Mound.

Earlier that day, Itabi had realized that there was something missing. His neck was bare where the emerald necklace had always been. He thought back— the last time he remembered having it was when White Raven Woman had guided him to the wolfpack.

Had he lost it, somehow, when he joined them in song? Itabi had felt himself go into panic and dismay. *I can't have lost it now, what will I do?* Anytime that he had lost faith in himself, all he had to do was clutch the emerald stone, and his faith was restored.

The understanding struck him like an avalanche. Bearcloud had given Itabi the necklace when he needed it; now, he no longer *had* a need for it. The emerald stone was a part of who he was, or, said in a different way, faith was the only ornament he needed.

He mounted the Emerald Mound barefoot, with the husk of corn from Dancing Bear Creek in one hand. He locked eyes with Wolf's Friend and recognition passed between the two. The men were chanting softly now, in unison. Itabi reached the top and paused to catch his breath.

Slowly turning in a circle, the boy found himself level with the treetops, floating in a sea of oranges of *onafapi*. It felt like he and the chanting mikos were the only people in that elevated world of color and wind. Placing the husk of corn in front of him, Itabi sat down, facing the setting sun.

For a moment, nothing happened. Everything continued as it had been happening. The boy saw this and felt content, allowing his heart to become centered on the Mound. He thought of all the guides that had crossed his path.

He felt the love of his mother and the energy of the Sun-Dancers; the forbearance of Ikbi and the vision of Running Hair; the courage of the first Fala and the second one with wings; the sensitivity of Anoli, the wisdom of Bearcloud, the wisdom of the wolves—all joined together.

Even Kallo, he reflected, had provided him the strength necessary to be *here*. The council's chant reached his throat. Something stirred around him. Opening his eyes, he saw that the *tanchi* had disappeared. Itabi felt a presence on the Mound and continued the chant.

211

The chant became a house in which he sat. Itabi found that there were words that spoke to him, faintly at first, and those words seemed to come from within. They said his name, and Itabi signaled that he had heard them. Another way of speaking, he thought to himself.

On whose authority do you seek us?

"The People of One Fire, *hacha hatak,* and their Seven Clans, who are missing the sacred fire."

How do you wish to rekindle the sacred fire?

"It is my understanding that there is a chant, the Emerald Chant, and that its medicine can heal our people and bless our lodges with the warmth of the Creator."

The Emerald Chant is a fortune of the humble, the foundation of ages of peace. Do you hold your voice in such a high esteem, that it may speak the essence of the stars?

"Only in proportion to what my heart is capable of, and what the People of One Fire need."

Your voice rises high as the Sun casts its rays. Do you continue to see yourself as less than worthy?

"I am equal to the great heights of my True Self, and the Dream it has granted me."

There will come a time when your world will suffer for the love it refused to give.

"We will embody the love it falls short of giving."

Have you recognized us?

"In the way that I recognize myself in the song of the wolves, the timelessness of the great river—yes, I have recognized you."

The men of the peace council heard none of this, but when they looked up at the boy from the Owl Clan, they saw a pillar of light stretching infinitely between the Mound and the darkening sky. They nudged each other and exchanged looks, but none dared interrupt the chant or call out his name. Its glare was like that of the sun.

There is a choice you must now make. You can keep the Emerald Chant for yourself, only sharing it with a select few. This will win you fame and enjoyment of human things. There is another path. You can spread the Emerald Chant freely to your people and revive the fires. In that case, you must leave them immediately after it is done — another journey will await you, and you alone.

I could never keep the chant from the people, the boy thought to himself. He had come to the Emerald Mound to restore peace and healing to the clans. What was a gift if only a few enjoyed it? Still, there was angst in his heart. Itabi knew that part of him desired being told that he was a hero, a *na lakonchi*. His old self, wounded from people's words, longed for that feeling.

But what about my True Self?

The pillar of light between the Emerald Mound and the sky flickered, faded—all was dark. Itabi stood up and walked over to where Colesqua was sitting. He whispered something in his ear. The Miko of the Owl Clan nodded and raised his arms for the singing to cease. The Earth, the Moon and the Sea all paused to listen at once. The elements stood suspended.

An ancient chant issued from Itabi's lips like a flash of silver turned into emerald, a chant that silenced the woodlands and brought with it memories, dreams and stories of the Great Spirit. Something surged into Being, at once old and new, something that was seeking the right instrument to sound its call. It was like rainfall for a garden of dreams.

The Miko placed a slab of basswood on the ground and sprinkled a handful of dried blossoms into the depression at its center. He then took a rod and, placing the end atop the tinder, slowly began rotating it between his palms. A wisp of smoke rose into the air, and then, like a rose, a small flame bloomed.

All of the men rushed to the top of the Emerald Mound at once. They crowded around Itabi and lifted him up onto their shoulders. The flame grew, an odor of burning pine reached their noses and their skin tingled with the familiar warmth, the warmth of their ancestors. They danced a dance of gratitude around the fire. Their joy ripened into song.

Way hey ya hey ya!

You a hey you ay!

A hey ya a hey ya!

Way hey ya hey ya!

You a hey you ay!

A hey ya a hey ya!

None of the men, in that moment, could have known that Itabi would be among the People of One Fire for only a short while longer. In all of the tales and legends that followed, he would become known simply as *Oti*, the fire-kindler. That was his new name, the name he received that very night in the company of his mikos, the name of which he was inexpressibly proud.

EPILOGUE

Wherever the Emerald Chant was sung, the sacred fires followed, and with them all of the forgotten traditions. The fighting between the clans immediately came to an end. A new age of harmony among the Seven Clans was ushered in and all the red banners were finally taken down.

With peace and prosperity restored, storytelling once more became the lifeblood of every *talwa*. The first story, of course, was always that of Oti, once known as Itabi. Wide-eyed children were taught how, if it weren't for Oti's great quest for the Emerald Chant, no fires would exist to cook their meals or warm their feet.

It was good to emulate the courage of Oti.

They learned how his mother, Opa, and Uncle Ikbi became man and wife, and settled down in the land where the great river emptied into the sea. They also learned how Running Hair's magic paintbrush gave her every color she wanted, and how she became the most renowned teacher of painting in the Clans.

Their scorn for Kallo, too, made them curious about his fate. After he was injured in the war, he returned to Chatelan and learned the ways of his grandfather, Shanafila. Kallo's medicine healed many an injured stickball player, although he himself never played again. It was Wolf's Friend who became the Miko of Chatelan at the time of Mishtubolih's death, and a wise Miko he was.

"But what about Oti, what about Oti," the children would demand, growing restless. After he toured every *talwa* of the Seven Clans with his enchanting song, Oti suddenly disappeared—no one knew where he went. Rumors spread that he had started another quest, a quest to visit the Sun to see where he slept.

Others thought that Oti had joined Bearcloud to carry out the will of the brothers in the sky. No one knew for sure, because he was never seen among the Seven Clans again—at least, not in human form. Many hunters told a tale, and it was always the same...

On a night around the time of the New Moon Festival, they would report seeing a pack of wolves. Among the gray wolves they would spot one that was different, a mighty wolf with a coat the color of the moon. It would lead the other wolves in song and, when it did, a white raven would appear and settle its wings nearby.

That was always the children's favorite story to hear, and when they fell asleep next to the fire, they invariably wore smiles on their faces.

Choctaw Glossary of Terms

Akat: Expression of agreement

Ankana: My friend

Busk: Original term for Green Corn Ceremony

Cassena: Also called 'White Drink,' it is a purgative drink consisting of holly

Hacha hatak: River people

Hale: Exclamation of distress

Halito: Hello

Hatak ikanumpolo: A mute person

Hatak inla: Foreign people

Hoke: Yes

Holhpokunna: A dreamer

Kia: Nevermind

Kwanoka'sha: A small forest spirit known for trickery

Mah!: An interjection used to get attention

Miko: Chief

Nakni tashka: Male warrior

Na lakonchi: Healer, savior

Onafapi: Autumn

Passa: A purgative drink consisting of button snakeroot

Talwa: Mississippian township

Tanchi: Corn

Yakoke: Thank you

Yamomahe alhpesa: Let it be so

Made in the USA
Monee, IL
15 September 2021